"You glow with happiness when you talk about the baby, you know."

Grace rested a hand protectively over her belly, admitting that she did feel an awesome, happy glow that seemed to radiate from the inside—and she hadn't even heard the baby's heartbeat or felt it move yet. "I never thought I'd be given the chance to have a child of my own."

"Of our own," Ford corrected mildly. "And I'm glad I could give you a baby. In fact, I'll give you as many as you want. After this baby is born, we can bend the rules a bit on the sleeping arrangements and work on number two."

His teasing tone prodded a tentative smile from Grace, but she had no idea what the future held for them. "How about we just take it one at a time?"

Dear Reader,

Back by popular request is our delightful series—
BABY BOOM. We've asked some of your favorite authors
in Harlequin Romance® to bring you a few more special
deliveries—of the baby kind!

In this story from Janelle Denison, the news of a baby on
the way comes as a complete surprise, but it also brings
together two people who were always meant for each other.
Join Ford and Grace as they prepare for that true labor of
love—parenthood!

**When two's company and
three's a family!**

THE BABY SURPRISE

Janelle Denison

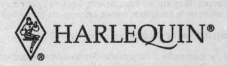

HARLEQUIN®

TORONTO • NEW YORK • LONDON
AMSTERDAM • PARIS • SYDNEY • HAMBURG
STOCKHOLM • ATHENS • TOKYO • MILAN • MADRID
PRAGUE • WARSAW • BUDAPEST • AUCKLAND

To my nieces, Brittany, Alisha and Brandi,
may you always follow your dreams
and find a happily-ever-after
of your own.

As always, to Don, for being my happily-ever-after.

ISBN 0-373-03614-0

THE BABY SURPRISE

First North American Publication 2000.

Copyright © 2000 by Janelle R. Denison.

Visit us at www.eHarlequin.com

Printed in U.S.A.

CHAPTER ONE

THE impact of colliding into such a solid wall of masculinity knocked the breath out of Grace Holbrook, and dazed her to the extent that she saw a few stars. It was as if he'd appeared out of nowhere, though she was sure he'd just come out of the bank, where she'd been heading. That's what she got for ogling the new brochures she'd just picked up from the printer's for her flower shop, instead of watching where she was going.

"Are you all right?"

His voice was deep, rich, and incredibly sexy, coaxing her back to the present with that direct pull on her feminine senses. Still feeling dazed, she blinked and slowly glanced up, summoning an apology for her clumsiness.

The words caught somewhere between her vocal chords and lips. He was a tall man, towering over her own five-foot-five frame with shoulders wide enough for a woman of her petite stature to completely lose herself in.

He was staring at her. At least she assumed he was watching her through the dark aviator sunglasses he wore. She couldn't see his eyes, and resented the fact that they concealed what appeared to be, by lack of original description, a drop-dead gorgeous face. What she could determine of his features were chiseled with strong lines and angles, except for his nose, which looked like it might have been

5

broken at one time. The slightly crooked slope, and those sensual, well-shaped lips of his, and thick, rich sable hair cut in a short, executive style, only served to accentuate his good looks.

Her admiration took in a hunter-green and beige patterned silk shirt, and tan pleated trousers that fitted to lean hips and thighs. Expensive Italian loafers completed his urban image.

He wasn't from around the small town of Whitaker Falls, Virginia, of that she was certain. For one, they didn't grow such sophistication, and second, word would have spread that a gorgeous new hunk had taken up residence nearby. Was he visiting someone?

"Are you still with me?" He tilted his head and smiled, producing a fascinating dimple at the corner of his mouth that flirted, charmed, and made Grace's breath hitch in her throat.

I know that dimple, that devastatingly seductive smile, she thought, then shook off the notion as absurd and a trick of her imagination. Her internal chastisement did little for the awareness fluttering in her belly.

"Since it seems I've knocked the breath out of you, maybe I ought to administer mouth-to-mouth?" he suggested, amusement evident in his voice. "I'd be happy to oblige…"

Her face flushed. "Yes. I mean no." She groaned in mortification. She couldn't remember the last time she'd been so flustered. Attempting to untie her tongue, she tried again. "*No* to the offer of resuscitation, and *yes,* I'm fine.

"I'm disappointed," he murmured.

Oh, so am I. Her gaze dropped to his lips, imagining the ways they could revive a woman. An all too familiar emptiness within her expanded to startling proportions.

She realized he was holding her upper arm; he must have steadied her when they'd collided. His grasp was gentle, his long fingers incredibly warm against her skin. Those same fingers that had offered her balance were tucked next to the side of her breast—innocently, of course, yet her pulse quickened erratically.

"I'm more embarrassed than anything," she said, for lack of something better to say. "I should have been paying more attention to where I was going."

"As I should have," he said, sharing half the blame.

His thumb stroked along her arm, an idle caress that caused another riot of sensations to bloom just beneath the surface of her skin. Unable to bear much more of the physical stuff, she eased her arm back, not unkindly, and he released her. The movement caused the strap of her purse to slide down her shoulder, jarring the arm carrying the brochures. Half of the printed material slid out of the protective plastic insert and fluttered to the brick sidewalk.

Groaning at yet another blunder, and in an attempt to conceal the heat creeping up her neck and over her face, she bent to retrieve the brochures. *Could this encounter get any worse, or any more humiliating,* she wondered.

He crouched beside her, picked up one of the brochures, but didn't hand it over. In fact, as she collected the mess she'd made, she grew uncomfortably aware of him watching her.

Tucking the last of the brochures back into the

protective insert, she glanced up, and found herself irritated by the sunglasses preventing her from really knowing him. She was certain his gaze was directed at her, but what *part* she couldn't be sure.

Uneasy under such intense private scrutiny, she grappled for something to say. "I'm okay, really," she told him, just in case his perusal was nothing more than the concern that she still might be feeling unstable. She almost laughed at that. Who was she kidding? He'd shaken up sensual emotions she'd long ago buried and had her thinking tempting, provocative things no sane woman would consider with a man she'd known less than five minutes.

"You're more than okay," he said, his voice low and husky. "You're absolutely beautiful."

Grace wanted to melt into a puddle at his feet, but that certainly wouldn't do. How could this man make her feel so special, so desired, with nothing more than three ordinary words? She'd never considered herself beautiful. Oh, she supposed she was pretty enough, but her simple beauty didn't inspire men to do double-takes. She wasn't voluptuous by any stretch of the imagination, but slender with gentle curves. She had thick, shoulder-length chestnut hair she normally wore up, or in a French braid, like today, and had inherited common brown eyes with little specks of gold in the center. Nothing distinctive or spectacular about her other facial features, either.

You have the sweetest mouth I've ever seen or tasted.

The eleven-year-old memory whispered through her mind. One man had appreciated that physical trait of hers, told her as much, and proved his reverence by spending hours teaching her all the sensual delights to be found with her mouth, and his.

She closed her eyes and shivered at the recollection, and along with the memories came the dull pain of loss, confusion, and a long-ago heartache that had never completely healed.

Why now?

"The compliment wasn't meant to cause you distress."

She opened her eyes, searching what she could of the man's face. That engaging smile again. That irresistible dimple. He was a stranger, yet...there was something familiar about him. Something she couldn't quite put her finger on. A connection she struggled to understand.

As if she'd scrutinized him longer than was comfortable, he straightened abruptly, breaking the silent contact and forcing her to stand, too, or remain staring at his knees.

She shifted the load in her arms, curiosity getting the best of her. "Have we met before?"

His expression revealed nothing, if in fact he had anything to hide. "I suppose, in another lifetime."

Was that a yes or no? His ambiguous answer frustrated her, and made her more determined to find out who he was. "Well, I guess I should introduce myself. I'm Grace Holbrook, the clumsy proprietress of Grace and Charm Flower Shop, located in Whitaker Town Square." Smiling, she offered her hand, a prompt for his own introduction. "And I promise I'm not nearly so clumsy with my customers' orders."

He laughed, a deep, throaty sound that did wonderful things to her nerve endings. Reaching out, he clasped her hand in his, but instead of giving it the brief shake she expected, he brought her fingers to his mouth and brushed the tips against his slightly damp lips.

"It's a pleasure," he murmured, his warm breath, the vibration of his voice, tickling her fingertips.

The unanticipated gesture stunned Grace. Her stomach dipped and tumbled and she experienced a moment of sheer light-headedness. The attraction between them was strong and undeniable... And dammit, she wanted to see his eyes, his entire face, without those sunglasses!

He moved her hand away from his lips, and his mouth curved into a mischievously wicked grin. "Maybe we'll run into each other again sometime."

His witty, double meaning wasn't lost on her. Her muddled brain just couldn't think of an equally clever response at the moment.

He nodded amicably, as if he hadn't just turned her inside out with a reckless, dangerous kind of wanting. "Have a good day, Ms. Holbrook." One of her brochures still in hand, he headed toward a champagne-colored luxury coupe she'd never seen before, his stride relaxed and confident.

As he slid inside the leather interior and pulled out of the parking slot, it occurred to Grace that the rogue hadn't given her his name.

Ford McCabe blew out a deep breath and glanced in his rearview mirror, catching one last glimpse of Grace Holbrook before she disappeared inside the bank where he'd just conducted his business. For all the ways he'd imagined a reunion with her, none of them had included literally bumping into her. And nothing had prepared him for the wave of emotion that had gripped him upon seeing her, or the heated desire that still flared between them. It had taken every ounce of willpower he possessed not to touch more than her hand, to kiss more than her fingers…to let his tongue taste the wild pulse he'd felt thrumming at her wrist.

To take off his sunglasses and shock the hell out of her.

Not knowing if she'd welcome him after so long, or scorn him for what had happened in the past, he refrained from doing something so spontaneous. But it hadn't stopped him from flirting, or spinning a web of sensuality she'd easily tangled herself in. She hadn't recognized him, but he'd had the advantage of wearing the sunglasses he'd just put on before exiting the bank, and years of a gradual, steady metamorphosis of spirit and body.

His physical appearance had altered greatly from the lanky, twenty-year-old rebel he'd been when he'd fled Whitaker Falls. Gone was the thick, dark brown hair he'd let grow to his shoulders and allowed the wind, or his fingers, to style. The years had darkened the strands to nearly sable; his tastes had changed to a short, no-nonsense precision cut that complemented the executive he'd become. His body had filled out to fit his gangly frame; racquetball and jogging had honed his muscles and kept him in shape. As for the expensive silk shirt and pleated trousers—no one who remembered Ford McCabe would associate him with anything less than faded, ripped jeans, tattered T-shirts, and tennis shoes held together with duct tape.

He'd come a long way in eleven years, driven by

a fierce determination to become something other than the illegitimate kid of a woman who'd lived her life in the depths of a bottle, and died in the same manner. Driven, too, to banish the haunting memories of his best friend's death, one man's all-consuming hatred, a town's criticism, and the sweet love of a girl he could never have.

No matter how hard he worked or the successes he'd achieved despite his impoverished upbringing, exorcizing any of those personal demons had been impossible, because they all linked to the one person he couldn't forget: Grace Holbrook, a woman who was lovelier than he remembered in his dreams. While an entire town spurned him for a heritage he'd been unfortunate enough to be born into, she'd been the one person who'd accepted him.

Shaking off those unsettling recollections, he set his mind back to his encounter with Grace. She'd introduced herself using her maiden name. Since he hadn't seen a ring on her left hand—and he'd defi-nitely looked—he assumed she was single, which amazed him. He'd honestly thought she'd be mar-ried by now, with the half a dozen kids she'd talked about having tagging alongside her.

It didn't mean she wasn't involved with someone, though he doubted as much. A woman in love didn't respond to another man the way she had to him that afternoon. He'd wanted her eleven years ago, and he wasn't all that surprised to realize he ached for her still. Considering the spark still evident between them, he intended to pursue the possibility of some-thing more.

Glancing at the passenger seat of his car to the Grace and Charm Flower Shop brochure he'd deliberately taken from Grace, he smiled, an impulsive idea forming in his mind. Instead of heading straight toward the hotel he was staying at, he made a left turn at the edge of Oakton Avenue, toward Whitaker Town Square.

It was time to set his eleven-year-old plan into motion. He was back in Whitaker Falls to claim what was rightfully his, and to prove that he *belonged*. He couldn't think of a more pleasant way to begin his adventure than stating his intentions to Grace with an outrageously lavish and romantic gesture.

Grace loved flowers. From the most elegant roses, tulips and lilies, to the simple wildflowers that grew in the fields on the outskirts of Whitaker Falls. She loved their vibrancy and lush scent, and how a simple bouquet could brighten someone's day and make them feel special.

Her business gave her an everyday opportunity to share her joy of flowers, and to surround herself with the beauty of nature's gift to earth. Opening a flower shop was a dream she'd had since she was a little girl, a goal inspired by a mother who'd loved growing her own flowers and tending the enormous garden that had once been behind their home. Now, at the age of twenty-nine, Grace and Charm was the focal point of Grace's life.

Two hours after her run-in with the gorgeous stranger, Grace pulled her van into a vacant slot in front of her shop, mentally chastising herself for checking the area for a champagne-colored vehicle, or the tall, dark-haired, sexy man she couldn't seem to get out of her mind. Neither car nor man were around, much to her disappointment—most likely he was already heading back to where he'd come from, their encounter forgotten.

Sighing, she gathered her briefcase, brochures and the other items she'd picked up after a Saturday morning spent running errands and visiting with her father, Dr. Ellis Holbrook. It was her weekly routine, her day to get caught up on banking and business related tasks she didn't have time for during the week. Dora Jenkins, her twenty-two-year-old employee, worked the morning shift on Saturdays, and Grace closed up by four in the afternoon, after the weekend business was ordered and delivered. Sundays she was closed—it was her one day to indulge herself and do as she pleased.

The bell above the glass door tinkled as she entered the establishment. Dora grinned as she walked out of the long, glass-enclosed refrigerating unit where they stored their supply of fresh-cut flowers. Carrying a bucket of bright yellow calla lilies and deep red dahlias, she brought them to the sturdy wooden workbench dominating the area just behind the front counter.

"Afternoon, boss," Dora greeted, her brown eyes sparkling cheerfully. She wore her blond hair in a pony tail, and a lavender apron over her T-shirt and jeans, the front of which was embroidered with the shop's name and a colorful bouquet of flowers.

"Hi, Dora." Grace gave the fresh flowers in the cooler a cursory glance as she passed, a habit that helped her keep a mental inventory of what she had, what she was low on and what she needed to order. The flowers were categorized in plastic buckets of water by type of blossom and foliage, and then grouped by color.

Her gaze stopped at the section where she stocked the long-stemmed roses. Yesterday afternoon before closing she'd noted over twelve dozen, in a variety of colors, and had planned to use the excess blooms in the basket arrangements and centerpieces she made up on Mondays for Whitaker Country Club's standing weekly order.

Amazed that she'd sold out of the expensive roses, she shook her head and pushed through the low swinging gate that separated the work area from the gift part of the boutique, where she displayed gift baskets, figurines, cards and other specialty items. She set a white bag on a side counter along the back wall—lunch from Gertie's Cafe for the both of them, another Saturday routine Grace had established.

"You've been busy this morning," Grace commented, though it was obvious by the excess foliage, cut stems and unusable flowers littering the workbench that Dora had been going crazy with orders. Not that Grace was going to complain about the extra sales. At seventy-five dollars a dozen, the cost of those roses alone could practically cover her month's rent.

"Um, very." Dora clipped the end of a calla lily and pushed the stem into the floral arrangement she was creating. "I've been going nonstop since I opened the doors this morning. In fact, this is the first chance I've had to start on the centerpiece Mrs. Thorne ordered for her dinner party tonight."

Grace headed toward the small office in the back to put her purse and briefcase away, along with the brochures she'd picked up from the printers. "I'll deliver it on my way home this afternoon." She opened the door, stepped inside her office, and came to an abrupt halt.

Dozens of long-stemmed roses, in every shade she'd had available, were displayed in the most elegant, crystal cut vases she offered her customers—at a substantial extra charge. The mild warmth of the room coaxed the tight buds to open and bloom and release their rich, intoxicating fragrance.

Grace's hand fluttered to her chest in dismay. Dora knew to keep arrangements—especially roses!—in the refrigerator until the customers picked them up. Within a few hours the roses would be completely open, but the unfurling process was for the customer to enjoy. She was looking at hundreds of dollars in merchandise that should have been in the cooler—and that thought was enough to give her a mild heart attack.

Setting her armload of items down on her desk chair—which was the only space that wasn't occupied by a vase of flowers—she retraced her steps back to the front of the shop.

"Dora, what are all those roses doing in my office?"

The young woman glanced up from sorting through stalks of pale purple delphiniums, a huge grin spreading across her face. "They're for you."

"Excuse me?" Grace was certain she'd misunderstood.

Efficiently clipping the stem of a delphinium, Dora poked it into the arrangement. "It's true. Every single one of those roses are yours. Bought and paid for by the most gorgeous man I've ever seen in Whitaker Falls.''

Confused, Grace slowly rounded the workbench and stood across from Dora. Who in the world would do something so outrageously extravagant for her? She'd dated a few men since her divorce five years ago, but there had never been anyone serious enough to inspire such a lavish, romantic gesture.

And none of those men would qualify as gorgeous status.

She frowned. ''Was it someone I know?''

''Oh, I sure do hope so,'' Dora said on a dreamy sigh. ''Though I have to admit I've never seen him around town. He left a card in one of the arrangements. Why don't you go see for yourself who they're from?''

''I'll do that.'' Intrigued, she headed back to her office, once again overwhelmed by the display of flowers, and the lush, seductive fragrance teasing her senses. It was strange, she thought as she searched each vase for a note. For as much as she loved brightening other people's lives with flowers, no one had ever sent her a bouquet before, let alone dozens of roses.

It was a heady, thrilling experience.

Finally finding a tiny white envelope nestled in a dozen elegant white roses, she plucked it out of the tangle of baby's breath and fern, and withdrew the florist card inside.

> I enjoyed bumping into you today, and would like to see you again. How about dinner tonight? Whitaker Country Club. 7:00 p.m.

The note wasn't signed, but there was no mistaking the identity of the mystery person—her gorgeous stranger. Grace's pulse thrummed in anticipation at the thought of accepting his dinner invitation, and she was quickly plagued by uncertainty. For as much as she was attracted to him, she knew nothing about the man except that he owned a smile that made her want to follow him anywhere, and breathtaking dimples that made her weak-kneed. Captivating charm and charisma hardly qualified as trustworthy...though he had seemed very respectable and pleasant.

"So, are you going to meet him for dinner?"

Grace jumped at the sound of Dora's voice from just behind her, as she read the note over Grace's shoulder. Turning, she stuffed the card back into the envelope. "I don't even know the man! He's someone I literally bumped into while I was going to the bank."

"So what," Dora said with a nonchalant shrug and a twinkle in her eye. "There comes a time in every woman's life when she ought to live a little on the edge."

Grace rolled her eyes at that, but oh, how she was tempted! For too long she'd been straitlaced and conservative in her choice of men, trying to gain her father's forgiveness for getting involved with the one boy the entire town had labeled as "no good white trash" and "nothing but trouble."

She bit her bottom lip, struggling with what she knew she *should* do, and what she *wanted* to do. "I don't know..."

Dora playfully flicked the end of Grace's French braid. "Let down that hair of yours for once and do something spontaneous,'' she urged. ''You'll be in a public place, surrounded by people you've known all your life. If you don't feel comfortable with him you can always call it an early night. And if the chemistry is really good between the two of you, you can always call it an early night.'' She followed up that double entendre with a sassy wink.

Grace laughed and shook her head. She'd never been promiscuous in her life, and she didn't intend to start now—no matter how sexy the man. ''You're outrageous.''

''And you desperately need a night out, without your father as your date.''

Grace heard the wry humor in Dora's voice, but knew her friend was being much more serious than she let on. Though she enjoyed having dinner with her father—she hated the thought of him living alone and eating by himself—she had to admit that he was the only man in her life as of late, which was pretty pathetic as far as her own love life was concerned. But lately, even her father had been encouraging her to ''get out and date more often.''

She was certain her father hadn't meant a stranger, but had more in mind one of the respectable, eligible bachelors in town—none of which appealed to Grace.

Taking a deep breath filled with the sensual, delicious scent of roses filling her office, Grace made the spontaneous decision to do something for herself, without her father's approval, and without worrying about what other people might think.

She turned to Dora with a smile that wiped away any lingering uncertainties. ''I'm going to meet my mystery man and find out exactly who he is.''

"Great!" Dora's enthusiasm was infectious. "Now we just need to find something for you to wear other than one of your conservative dresses or button-up business suits."

Before Grace could take offense to that, Dora eyed her with a sly smile of a woman confident in her ability in attracting men. "I saw the perfect dress for you in the window of Shalimar's. I'm going to call Andrea right now and let her know that we'll be there as soon as we close up shop for the day."

As Dora exited the small office, Grace was overwhelmed with the notion that for the first time in a very long time she was actually excited about something other than the joy her business brought her.

She was excited about seeing a man.

CHAPTER TWO

BUTTERFLIES swarmed in Grace's belly as she entered the Whitaker Country Club at precisely 7:00 p.m. and walked up to the maître d's podium. Alfred, the astute man who'd served as host to the country club for as long as Grace could remember, smiled amicably when he saw her.

"Good evening, Ms. Holbrook," he greeted, his tone as warm and polite as his kind blue eyes. "You look positively lovely tonight."

The enthusiastic compliment caused her cheeks to warm, especially since the deep purple fitted dress, complete with black-hued stockings and black heels, was a far cry from the more conservative outfits she wore while dining at the country club with her father. Though the sleeves were long, the soft velvet material hugged her curves to her knees.

"Thank you, Alfred." Feeling a bit self-conscious, she refrained from tugging at the hem of her dress, or touching the soft curls cascading from the clip securing her thick hair atop her head. The few strands that had escaped her attempt at a sophisticated style tickled the side of her neck.

She clutched her little black purse tighter in her hand. "I'm meeting with someone at seven. Has he arrived?"

Alfred acknowledged her question with a curt nod. "Yes, right this way, Ms. Holbrook."

Instead of heading toward the main dining room,

he guided her down a wide corridor that led to a wing of small, private rooms normally reserved for intimate gatherings, which were rented out at an additional fee.

Realizing she would be completely alone with this stranger, instead of surrounded by familiar faces in the main dining room as she'd originally thought, she caught Alfred's jacketed arm when he reached for the doorknob of the "Crystal Room."

He lifted a bushy, salt-and-pepper brow in inquiry.

"Did the gentleman give you his name?" she asked quietly.

That earned her an odd look from Alfred, as if she should have known who she was meeting. "No, Ms. Holbrook, and he reserved the room under your name. Would you like me to find out his name for you?"

Feeling foolish under Alfred's concerned scrutiny, she quickly shook her head. "No, I'll be fine."

"Very well." He opened the door and waited until she stepped into the room, which she did, very tentatively. "If you need anything you can use the intercom on the wall, or the one on your table. Enjoy your evening." He executed a curt bow, then was gone, closing the door behind him.

Standing at the back of the room, Grace waited for her eyes to adjust to the dim lighting of the overhead chandelier. Gradually the furnishings came into focus, revealing a small, intimate room. A dining table sat in the middle of the area, just beneath the chandelier, set for two with linen, crystal, gold-rimmed china, gleaming silverware and one of her flower arrangements. Two tapered candles glowed cozily in the middle of the table, adding to the romantic atmosphere. Moonlight shimmered from outside the open sliding glass door, which led to a balcony overlooking the golf course.

And that's when she saw him, standing at the black wrought-iron railing enclosing the balcony, his back to her. He wore a navy-blue jacket that stretched across his broad shoulders and tapered to a trim waist, and gave way to matching trousers. His dark hair gleamed with moonlight, and she had the sudden giddy thought that she'd finally get to see his face, his eyes.

Slowly she set her purse on the edge of the table, summoning the nerve to break the silence that was making her more anxious by the minute.

"Hello," she said softly.

She saw his body tense ever so slightly, then after a hesitant second he turned around. Her gaze remained on his face, and though the light from inside the room cast a silhouette over him, his features, unobstructed by the sunglasses he'd worn earlier, were unmistakable.

Her breath caught painfully in her chest. Her heart seemed to stop beating, then resumed at a maddening pace. She took a step back, feeling as though she'd seen an apparition from her past—one who'd grown into an exceptionally good-looking man, and had the grace and manners of a polished gentleman.

Ford McCabe.

The last time she'd seen him had been at her brother's funeral, eleven years ago. She'd been all of eighteen, Ford twenty. Once the services were over, he'd left Whitaker Falls without saying goodbye or ever contacting her.

He'd broken her heart. According to her father, Ford McCabe had shattered their lives.

"Ford?" she whispered, hope mingling with the heartache she'd carried around for so long.

Gradually he closed the distance between them, leaving the evening shadows behind. Stunned, she could only watch, until finally he stood an arm's length away and looked down at her with rich, violet-colored eyes, and the tentative beginnings of a dimple creasing his lean cheek.

"Hello, Grace."

Ford stared into Grace's luminous brown eyes brimming with shock and disbelief, and waited anxiously for a response. A deep, vital part of him feared the possibility of her rejecting him, and that emotion had him all tangled up in knots.

He'd known when he'd made the decision to return to Whitaker Falls that the young girl he'd loved and left behind might have grown to hate him, and in some ways, he couldn't blame her if she had. He'd been a wild, selfish kid, consumed with his own hatred and bitterness, and torn between believing he deserved someone as sweet and unassuming as her and knowing he had nothing to offer in return. She'd been the only gentle, kind thing in a life surrounded by the disgrace of his uncaring, drunk of a mother. His character had been tainted as white trash right from the cradle, and he hadn't stood a chance to redeem himself, not when everyone automatically thought and expected the worst from "that wild McCabe boy." Living up to the reckless reputation the town had labeled him with had been easier to do than struggling for the respect and acceptance he'd always craved.

He'd returned to his home town to gain that respect and acceptance, and it all started here and now, with Grace.

He tilted his head, and attempted to lighten the moment. "I suppose you have every reason to be shocked. After all, this is a first."

Her expression clouded over with confusion, and much to his disheartenment, her demeanor turned cool and distant. "What's a first?" she asked, eyeing him warily.

He spread his hands wide, presenting the wealthy man he'd become. "Seeing Ford McCabe within the walls of the Whitaker Country Club." His voice was low and teasing, meant to cajole a smile from her.

Her rigid posture relaxed a fraction, but no smile. "I suppose it is," she agreed, her gaze flicking over him, absorbing the changes from skinny, rebellious boy to a distinguished grown man. "It looks like you've come a long way since leaving Whitaker Falls."

"I have." Seeing the barrage of questions in her eyes that he wasn't ready to answer, he decided to cut them off at the pass. His gaze encompassed the expensively furnished room. "I have to admit that the accommodations here are outstanding. Better than I ever imagined. Will you stay and have dinner with me?"

He held his breath while she thought over his question, and let it out in a quiet rush when she finally made her decision.

"Yes, I'll stay."

Relief washed over him. "I'm glad."

An awkward silence settled between them. Shifting on her feet, she smoothed a slender hand down the front of her dress in a nervous gesture. His gaze followed the movement, entranced by the lush, womanly curves she'd developed over the years. She was still petite and slender, but her breasts were fuller than before, her hips more gently rounded. Her legs looked as gorgeous as ever, lithe and toned, and graceful as a dancer's. Heat curled through him—as a teenage boy, he'd spent hours fascinating about those limbs, that lissome body, and he wasn't surprised to realize she affected him just as powerfully as she had in his youth.

He lifted his eyes to hers, and for the first time their gazes connected, spiraling him back in time, then fast-forwarding him to the present again. All the lonely years in between crashed in on him, and before he could stop himself, words were spilling from his mouth.

"I've missed you, Grace," he said huskily, the sentiment honest and straight from a part of himself he'd kept sealed off to anyone who tried to get close to him. "More than you could ever know. For eleven years, you're all I ever thought about."

Her eyes widened, and he saw her tightly woven emotions unraveling, softening—banishing the last of her reserve. "I missed you, too, Ford."

A smile tipped his mouth, and immense pleasure washed over him at her admission, which bolstered his confidence and gave him hope for what lay ahead. Giving into the temptation to touch her, he wound his finger around one of the silken curls escaping her upswept hair, and was gratified when she didn't pull away.

Caught up in the notion that he might have consumed her thoughts as much as she had his, he couldn't resist prompting her for more. "Yeah?"

She nodded, and shivered delicately when the pad of his finger strummed gently along the side of her neck. He expected her to say more about missing him, but those trusting eyes of hers that he'd never forgotten locked on his, shimmering with a more painful accusation. "You left without saying goodbye."

His hand stilled at her collarbone. Fell away. The injured note in her voice struck him right in the midsection, making him realize she still harbored a wealth of hurt from his past actions. His reasons for leaving Whitaker Falls so abruptly had come on an overwhelming revelation that had left little room for goodbyes. As long as he remained in the small town where he'd grown up and made a disreputable name for himself, he'd never amount to anything—no would give him the chance to prove that he *could* change, that beneath all his recalcitrant behavior there were redeeming qualities crying to be recognized and nurtured.

He'd attempted to modify his rebellious ways and wild habits, all in the hope of being respectable enough for Grace Holbrook. But one fateful night had destroyed all his own personal hopes and dreams, forcing him to escape the condemnation that had spread through the community of Whitaker Falls. He could only hope eleven years was enough time to heal the wounds of the past.

"I'm sorry," he said softly, knowing the apology was little compensation for what he'd done to her.

She graciously let that go, but if he expected a

relaxing evening with her, she had other things in mind. She circled around the table, putting it between them. "Why didn't you tell me that it was you outside of the bank today? You acted as though we didn't know each another."

Figuring they both could use a glass of champagne, he withdrew the chilled bottle from the silver ice bucket next to the table, and popped the cork. "The incident caught me by surprise, and I wasn't ready to reveal who I was just then." Pouring two flutes of the bubbly liquid, he set a glass at each of the place settings. Then he pulled out one of the cushioned chairs and motioned for her to sit.

Sliding into the seat he offered, her eyes narrowed, the depths glowing golden from the candlelight on the table. "You led me to believe you were a stranger!"

Taking the chair across from her, he smiled, enjoying her fiery display of temper, which he knew stemmed more from frustration than anger. "Maybe, but I was being completely truthful when I said you were absolutely beautiful."

That took the wind out of her sails, and she sat back in her chair. Her tongue swept across her bottom lip, and she appeared startled by her own provocative action. "I'm not beautiful," she refuted, sounding prim. "Pretty, maybe, but hardly beautiful."

He wanted to laugh at how guileless she still was about her appearance. "At eighteen, you were pretty, but you've grown into a beautiful woman." He could see the doubt in her expression, and found it difficult to believe another man hadn't seen and appreciated all that she was. "And you still have the most sensual mouth I've ever seen, with full, soft, kissable lips.''

He could have sworn he saw her pulse flutter at the base of her throat. "Ford—"

"I couldn't get enough of your mouth, your kisses,'' he went on, making her remember exactly what they'd shared, and how good it was. "It's hard to believe I was the first boy to teach you how to French kiss, but I do have to say that you were a quick learner, and a very receptive student.'' The hours they'd spent perfecting those slow, deep kisses had nearly driven him out of his mind, but had taught him the true anticipation of waiting for something infinitely more special. Restraint had been his own lesson that lazy spring afternoon. "Do you remember that day, Grace?"

She blushed furiously in answer. "Yes,'' she murmured, and reached for her flute of champagne, taking a gulp.

"I've relived that day, those kisses, a thousand times in my mind since leaving Whitaker Falls,'' he said, his fingers stroking along the stem of his champagne glass, his gaze holding hers. "You were so incredibly generous, and sweet. Sweeter than anything I've ever had in my life, then or since.''

He watched her visibly swallow, saw her struggle to keep her composure. "That was a long time ago, Ford.''

"Yet it seems like yesterday,'' he said, then let the trip down memory lane linger between them. Pressing the button on the intercom next to his place setting on the table, he let their waiter know they were ready to begin dinner.

Grace took another drink of her champagne,

studying him over the rim. "So, what is this private room all about?"

"I wanted to see you, and talk with you, without prying eyes watching our every move, and eaves-droppers listening to our conversation." An easy smile curved his mouth. "Is it so wrong to want this night alone with you?"

She seemed to consider that, then ducked her head sheepishly. "I have to admit that I'd be feeling quite uncomfortable right about now if we were in the main dining room."

"Exactly," he said drolly. "No sense stirring up unnecessary trouble."

Her delicately arched brow shot upward at the word "trouble." "Does anyone else know you're in town, other than me?"

He caught the subtle drift of worry in her expression, and wondered if she was thinking about her father, and the possibility of *him* discovering Ford McCabe was back in town. While he'd been conducting his business in the bank he'd received a few speculative stares, as if those few people were trying to place him, but no one had confronted him. Through idle chitchat he'd learned the young woman who'd helped him with his transaction had transferred from Richmond, Virginia, and was engaged to Eddie Logan, a local. She hadn't been around during Ford's scandalous years, so the business and personal residence information he'd divulged hadn't made any difference to her. He hadn't recognized the woman in Grace's shop, and since he'd paid cash for all those roses, he hadn't given her his name. Though he'd been careful about keeping his return low-key for now, it was inevitable that everyone learn the truth, sooner or later.

He just preferred later.

He shrugged lazily in answer to her question. "You're the only person I've contacted since arriving in Whitaker Falls."

She digested that as their waiter arrived with fresh salads and warm, crusty bread. Once the man had disappeared again, she slathered a slice of bread with butter, her eyes transferring from the task, to him.

"What brings you to Whitaker Falls?"

He winked playfully at her. "I was passing through on business, and thought I'd stop and see an old friend." Another vague half-truth, but he wasn't quite ready to reveal his true plans until he figured out where he stood with her.

She laughed, the light sound touching an empty part of his soul. "Well, this is certainly a surprise."

He stabbed his salad with his fork. "A good or bad surprise?"

"An unexpected one," she said prudently, as if she hadn't decided what to make of his impromptu visit. "How long will you be in the area?"

"Until tomorrow." He'd attended to his business in Whitaker Falls, but had to return to his company in Richmond for the week. From there, he'd play it by ear, depending on Grace, and his reception in Whitaker Falls. "I'm staying at the Hampton Inn for tonight."

The waiter returned, this time with their main course of rack of lamb, buttered potatoes and seasoned vegetables. Neither one spoke as the young man served them, and the silence gave Grace time to observe Ford from across the table.

Now that the initial shock of seeing him had worn off, she had a hundred questions for him, which he was answering—though there was no mistaking that he was selecting his responses very carefully. She supposed he had every right to be discreet, considering his past and the reputation he'd left behind, but she wanted more than the superficial information he offered. His obscure line about "passing through on business" certainly sparked her interest, but she wasn't one to push what he wasn't ready to willingly volunteer. Just as she had her reservations about his arrival in town, she was sure he had his reasons for being here. But it did make her wonder about his motives—was he driven by curiosity, or the "business" he spoke of? And what kind of "business" could he possibly have in Whitaker Falls?

She swallowed a bite of tender lamb, and chased it down with a sip of champagne. The bubbles tickled the back of her throat and warmed her belly, relaxing her. "So, what have you been up to all these years? They've certainly been good to you."

Something flashed in his eyes, pride mingling with caution. "It didn't begin that way, as you could well imagine. When I left Whitaker Falls I went to Richmond and took a job with a development firm. I started out as a laborer, doing grunt jobs on construction sites, and gradually worked my way up in one company to project manager."

She waited, but he offered no more than that morsel of information. "I'm happy for you, that you're doing so well."

Finished with his meal, he set his fork and knife

on his plate. "And what about you? You've got your own flower shop now. Nice place, by the way." He grinned, producing that sensual dimple of his, making her stomach dip with awareness.

She smiled back though she got the distinct impression he was turning the tables on her, making her the focus of their conversation, instead of him. "Grace and Charm certainly keeps me busy."

He refilled both of their glasses with more champagne. "And your father, how is he doing?"

Grace paused before answering. Under normal circumstances, she would have accepted his query about her father as an ordinary one—but the question seemed so incongruous, considering the fact that her father despised Ford, and the man across from her knew that, too. But as she looked into Ford's deep, dark violet eyes, she saw no signs of harbored ill feelings toward Ellis Holbrook, just sincere interest.

Dabbing her mouth with her napkin, she set the cloth on her plate, and pushed the dish aside. "My dad is doing well. He's still working as a family practitioner, part-time mostly. You remember Dr. Chase, my father's partner, don't you?" At Ford's nod, she continued. "He'll probably take over the practice when dad retires, which will hopefully be soon."

"And your mother?"

A pang of sadness struck Grace, and she wondered if missing her mother would ever go away. Apparently, Ford didn't know that Felice Holbrook had passed away within a year of her son's death, or that her father blamed Ford for that incident as well. "She's been dead over ten years now," she said quietly, keeping her explanation short and precise and skimming the more devastating details of her mother's passing. "She died of a severe strain of pneumonia."

"Ahhh, Grace, I'm so sorry." Genuine regret deepened his voice. Standing, he came around to her side of the table and offered her his hand. "Come on, I think we could both use some fresh air." He nodded toward the open slider leading to the balcony.

She agreed, and settled her small hand in his much larger, warmer one. It felt as if he was engulfing her, physically and emotionally. Odd, she thought, that he could return after eleven years and slip under her skin so easily again. For as much as he'd hurt her with his abrupt departure, for as much as they'd both changed in the time he'd been gone, she still felt that crazy affinity with him—as if he was "the one." A foolish notion, she knew, obviously left over from her youth when she'd believed in happy endings, white knights and happily-ever-afters. Now, she was a grown woman—experience having taught her to be practical in her expectations about men, romance and forever promises.

Out on the balcony it was dark, illuminated only by the glow of the moon. Letting go of Ford's hand, Grace curled her fingers around the railing and took a deep breath of fresh, chilled April air, clearing her head and lungs. Though they could hear the sounds of people talking and laughing from the dining room a few balconys down, she and Ford seemed to be cocooned in their own solitary world. Grace preferred it that way—not only was she enjoying their privacy, but she had no wish to deal with curious stares and whispers behind her back. There was no need for anyone to know her business, or that she'd spent the evening with Ford McCabe.

Especially her father.

"Things sure have changed since I've been gone," Ford commented idly, pushing his hands into his trouser pockets. "And then some things haven't changed at all."

She regarded him curiously. "You mean the people?"

"The entire town. Whitaker Town Square is new, and a much-needed, modern addition to the town, if you ask me. Yet Frankie and Earnest still sit out in front of the barber shop, playing their game of chess while watching the world go by."

She refrained from commenting that Frankie and Earnest's daily ritual might end soon, depending on what the new landowner of that strip of stores decided to do with the property. "Did you stop and say hello?"

"No." He grinned an adorably impish grin. "I'm not sure if they're still holding a grudge for the time I rode by on my bike and threw a bunch of firecrackers next to them and nearly gave them both a heart attack."

Grace laughed at the old memory, but clearly remembered the outrage that had followed on the heels of that prank. What Ford had done had been foolish and dangerous, no doubt, but when she'd told her mother of the incident, Felice had just sadly shaken her head. While everyone condemned Ford, her mother made the comment that the act of rebellion was a cry for attention. At the time, Grace hadn't understood how a perilous stunt could be construed as such, until she'd met Ford face-to-face and she'd seen the hostility in his eyes, and the pain and loneliness of a lost little boy. And despite her father's warnings to stay away from that "no good McCabe boy," Grace had made it her personal crusade to befriend him and accept him when the rest of the town scorned him.

Never would she have guessed she'd fall in love with him.

Blowing out a deep breath, she thought about all the different things that had remained the same in his absence, and the other things that had changed. Like the place where he grew up.

"Ford, I don't know if you realize this yet or not, but…have you been out to Cutter Creek?"

"Yeah, I've been there." His expression remained unreadable as he commented on the land where he'd lived the first twenty years of his life. "Quite an impressive house someone built there."

Impressive was an understatement for the huge, sprawling ranch-style home, complete with barn, corral and all the amenities to accommodate livestock. "The house is certainly the gossip of Whitaker Falls."

Amusement glimmered in his eyes. "Really?"

"Rumor has it that FZM, Inc. bought the land. Whoever that is tore down the original house and barn to build what's there now." She waited for him to confirm or deny the speculation, if he in fact knew anything at all. The property had gone into foreclosure shortly after his mother had passed away, which had been only a few months before Ford had left town.

"Amazing what money can buy, hmm?" he

drawled, a sarcastic bite to his tone. "Has anybody met the new owner yet?"

"No, and the construction crew who built the place didn't seem to know who the landowner was, either. Everything went through FZM. The house is completed, so I suppose it's just a matter of time before we meet the new resident."

Since Ford made no reply, Grace assumed he knew nothing about the person who'd purchased the land that had belonged to his grandfather. The property had been passed down to his mother, Candace, only to be mortgaged to the hilt to support her drinking and carousing habits, leaving Ford with nothing.

The orchestra in the dining room struck up a tune, and the music floated out the French doors and carried on the breeze, curling around the two of them. A faint, wistful look touched Ford's expression as he gazed out at the darkened golf course, though for the life of Grace she couldn't imagine what had captured his attention. The man was shrouded in secrets, an enigmatic puzzle she couldn't quite piece together. For as much as they'd shared in the past few hours, she felt as though he was holding back twice as much, and she couldn't help but wonder about all that he *wasn't* revealing.

"It's so strange to stand here and look out over the golf course." His voice was quiet, and strangely humbled.

Grace took in the strong lines of Ford's profile, his sensual mouth and firm, still-stubborn jaw. "Why is that?"

"Because I'm used to being on the other side," he said simply.

Her chest expanded, hurting for him and the outsider he'd been as a child. She'd never thought of how the town appeared from his perspective, but she wanted to know now. "Tell me."

"When I was a kid, I'd sit out on the golf course after dark, right over there on that hill by the thirteenth hole," he said, pointing in that direction and leading her gaze toward that dark, secluded spot. "I'd stay there for hours, looking through those open French doors leading into the dining room of the country club, watching everyone eat their meals, and wonder what steak and lobster might taste like. And if I was real lucky, I'd see you and your family having dinner together." Slowly, he turned toward her, reached out and brushed back the curl fluttering against her cheek. His thumb caressed her jaw, lingering there, and his eyes all but consumed her. "I'd watch the couples dance, would sometimes see you in some gangly kid's arms, and would imagine what it would be like to dance with you, to hold you in *my* arms and sweep you off your feet. Pretty ridiculous, huh?"

She never knew, but could only imagine how detached he'd must have felt from the rest of the town, how isolated and bereft. Her throat was so tight, it ached, but she managed to answer him in a whisper, "No, not ridiculous at all."

He gave her a dubious look tempered with the charm he'd developed with maturity. "Only you wouldn't think so."

She could hardly make up for his deprived childhood, but at that moment, she wanted to give him something to make up for every dance he'd missed. That was something she could do.

Moving slowly, she placed her hands on his shirt-front, feeling the steady beat of his heart. Sliding her palms up around his neck, she gradually closed the distance between them. Masculine heat radiated from him, and firm muscles bunched beneath the caress of her hands. The air around them fairly crackled with awareness, and she reveled in the shimmer of desire coursing through her veins.

His incredible eyes took on a hot glow, and his hands automatically gripped her hips, keeping their bodies from melding completely. "What are you doing?" His voice was hoarse.

A feminine smile curved her mouth as the slow ballad from the dining room swirled seductively around them in the moonlight. "Relax and put your arms around me. I'm going to give you that dance."

CHAPTER THREE

FORD realized he didn't have much choice in the matter when it came to dancing with Grace, not when she'd plastered her slender body against his, determined to lead him in a slow, swaying kind of shuffle that was romantic, and very intimate. He wasn't about to complain about her bossy tactics; he'd dreamed of holding her just like this for eleven long years.

He slid his arms around her waist, and she snuggled up to him, her soft breasts crushing against his chest. Her thighs aligned to his, and a flood of heat ignited a swift current of desire in his groin. He drew a steady breath, and inhaled a light, feminine fragrance that reminded him of the scent he'd encountered when he'd entered her flower shop earlier that day—a heady combination of roses, and warm sensuality. The fragrance was intoxicating, and extremely arousing.

She looked up at him, her lashes half-mast, and a bewitching smile claiming her lips. "Have you been taking lessons while you've been gone?"

The teasing note to her voice warmed him deep inside. "Nope. You're just an exceptional teacher."

Her husky laughter mingled with the music, and she melted deeper into his embrace, resting her cheek against his chest. He was certain she could hear the stampede of his heart, the rush of blood in his veins. She curled closer and sighed contentedly.

The gesture was so trusting, so accepting, that he experienced a flash of guilt. He swallowed hard, and tried not to think about everything he *hadn't* told Grace. Not once had he outright lied to her during their conversation, but he was certainly culpable by omission.

But he couldn't bring himself to reveal his intentions. Not here. Not now. Not when his life was finally fulfilled and perfect, even if for just this one night. Not when he was so close to achieving every one of the aspirations that had driven him for eleven years.

Including Grace.

Closing his eyes, he let go of the past, didn't think about the future, and focused on the pleasure of the present. He smoothed his hand down the soft velvet covering her back, and she shivered in response. She lifted her head and looked up at him with lustrous brown eyes rimmed in the finest of gold. Her brow creased slightly, and he could see her fighting the attraction that had them both under its tantalizing spell.

His gaze dropped to her mouth, stirring old memories to life. Her lips parted, and the warmth of her breath caressed his jaw. Accepting the silent invitation before she changed her mind, he lowered his head and tentatively brushed his lips across hers, rediscovering the taste and texture of her. The kiss was so simple, so sweet, it made him ache in a place only she'd ever touched.

Her hands came to rest on the front of his shirt, but she didn't push him away. "Ford..." Her voice was wobbly, uncertain, and maybe a little scared of what was happening between them.

He understood. The magic was still there, that compelling, unexplainable sorcery that lured a man and woman together, no matter how wrong it might be. The magnetism defied logic, as well as wealth, or reputation, or compatibility.

It just was.

Curling a hand around the side of her neck, he used his thumb to tip her chin up, to keep her mouth beneath his. She didn't protest, physically or verbally, and instead leaned into him at the same time the hand at his nape pulled his head down. Her lashes fluttered closed just before he settled his mouth over hers. This time, there was nothing simple about the kiss. From the get-go, this was a lush, adult kiss, borne of passion, and fueled by emotion.

Her lips were warm, pliable, allowing him to do as he pleased. And he did. He took his time, savoring the glide of damp lips, relishing the silky slide of his tongue along hers, and reveling in the uninhibited way she returned the embrace. He craved the way she tasted, like a warm, lazy summer day.

An eternity later, when he finally ended the kiss, they were both breathing raggedly. Only one thought clouded his mind, and he expressed it. "What do you say we go somewhere more private?" His voice was low and rough with arousal, thick with need.

She blinked up at him, a hesitant frown touching her brow. True, he was dealing with a grown woman with sensual desires, not the young, shy girl he'd left behind, but Grace proved to be the cautious sort, not that he could blame her for that.

He caressed the back of his knuckles down her soft cheek. "I'd like to be alone with you."

She wanted that, too—but he could see the need warring with indecision in her eyes, could see her thinking about the implications of leaving with him. After a brief moment, the doubts seemed to clear and she asked, "Would you like to go to your place or mine?"

Her question gave him a moment's pause. He had no idea if she still lived with her father. "Define 'your place.'"

A grin quirked her mouth, as if she read his concern. "I live alone, if that's what you're wondering."

"Your place, then." The last thing he wanted was for Grace to be seen with him at the hotel where he was staying. He wanted her, yes, but not at the cost of her reputation. "Follow me back to the hotel so I can leave my car there."

She nodded, and he swooped down for another deep kiss that wiped away the last of any doubts and left them trembling and reluctant to part. He hoped the sensual rush lasted until they arrived at her place.

Tossing enough bills on the table to cover the tab and leave a generous tip, Ford ushered Grace out of the Whitaker Country Club.

The back way.

What in the world was she doing?

Grace pondered that question for the hundredth time as she cast a surreptitious glance at the man sitting in the passenger seat of her business van. He stared out his window as they turned left out of the heart of town and headed toward a remote part of Whitaker Falls. While her stomach tumbled with a combination of nerves and anticipation, he appeared calm. Ford wasn't a stranger, but she'd never taken a man to her place before.

She knew little about the successful, gorgeous man he'd become, but there was no denying her feelings for him still ran deep and strong. Overwhelmingly so.

She'd been alone for so long, she yearned to feel that special connection again, craved to take a chance on the irresistible passion that simmered between her and Ford. She'd been the good girl her father expected of her, catering to his whims and wishes and keeping the reputation of the family name intact, but tonight was hers. Tonight, the man who'd always held her heart was hers.

"Where is your place?"

Ford's deep, smooth voice soothed her frayed nerves and directed her attention to something other than her troubling thoughts. "It's about three miles up the way. Remember Hattie Morgan's cottage?"

The interior of the vehicle was dark, but she saw him nod. "Yeah, I remember. The only thing separating Cutter Creek from Hattie's was a half a mile of forest."

"The forest is still there," she confirmed. The house itself was secluded, in a copse of tall trees, and overlooked a crystal-blue lake. The area was quiet, peaceful, and gave her plenty of privacy instead of living in town. "Hattie died about four years ago, and I bought the place. The cottage is small, with only two bedrooms and a cozy living room, but it's perfect for just one person."

"I have to admit, I'm surprised that you're not married."

She glanced his way, momentarily caught up in

the intensity of his eyes before training her gaze back to the road. She didn't want to talk about David, not tonight, but she wasn't going to lie to Ford. "I was married, for almost five years."

He was quiet, and she could feel him staring at her. When he reached out and touched her, trailing his fingers over her shoulder, she felt an odd stirring of relief.

"What happened?" he asked.

"We married for all the wrong reasons." She shrugged, not willing to delve too deeply into those reasons with Ford, since he was one of them. "He moved to Norfolk after the divorce. I hear from his mother that David is remarried and has two little boys."

His finger flicked a soft curl laying against her neck. "You two didn't have any kids?"

"No. We tried, but it didn't work out for us." She squelched the painful reality that she'd been the one unable to conceive, and turned onto the gravel road that led to her cottage. She kept up a stream of inconsequential chatter to keep Ford from questioning her last comment, though she was certain he was smart enough to catch the drift of what she'd said. A minute later, she parked the van under an awning, and cut the engine.

"Well, here we are," she said brightly, and exited the vehicle. She met up with him on the cobblestone walkway leading to her porch, and more nervous chatter bubbled from her as she opened the door and they entered the small cottage.

The rich, luscious scent of roses assaulted her senses, making her feel even more light-headed and anxious than she already was. She'd left the light above the stove in the kitchen on, which provided a small amount of illumination to the room. She flipped a switch on the wall, and the living-room lamp flooded the area with bright, comforting light. Somewhere between the hotel and her cottage her confidence in following through on her romantic evening with Ford had fled.

He grinned when he saw all the crystal vases occupying the vacant space in her living room. Those dimples of his deepened with humor. "Wow," he murmured.

Setting her purse on the small table by the door, she stepped out of her heels. "I don't think I thanked you for all these roses."

His eyes crinkled at the corner. "It was my pleasure."

"It cost you a small fortune," she said, knowing exactly how much money he'd doled out for the flowers and the extravagant vases. "It was unnecessary, and certainly overkill."

He merely shrugged off the exorbitant amount as inconsequential, and rubbed a red rose petal between his fingers. "If I remember correctly, you always loved flowers, roses especially."

"I do." She was deeply touched that he remembered. "They remind me of my mother and all the time I spent helping her tend to her rose garden when I was a little girl." Her father had since replaced the rose garden with sod, because it had been too painful for him to look at the garden that had once been his beloved wife's. Needlessly, she fussed with an arrangement of tight, fragrant buds—anything to keep her busy and moving. "I have no idea what I'm going to do with so many dozens."

"Enjoy them."

Her mouth opened to reply, then snapped shut when she saw that he was making himself comfortable. Slipping out of his navy jacket, he draped it over the back of her floral sofa. He loosened his tie, and her stomach dipped.

"Can I get you something to drink?" she blurted, her voice high-pitched to her own ears. "Coffee? Juice? Wine?" She breezed past him toward the kitchen, and he caught her wrist, halting her progress.

His eyes were warm, and kind, and a tad amused. "I'm not thirsty."

"A slice of cheesecake, then? I bought a few slices from the bakery yesterday, and I even have fresh strawberries to top it off."

"I'm not hungry for dessert, either." His soft, low voice catered to her jumbled nerves. The way he stroked his thumb over the pulse point in her wrist sent a pleasant thrum of desire through her. "Would you rather I go back to my hotel?"

"No!" Startled by her sharp tone of voice, she cleared her throat. Despite wanting him, the good girl she'd been for so long was very nervous about the night ahead. "I mean, I want you to stay, it's just that...well..." Twin spots of heat burned her cheeks, and she looked away.

Tucking a finger beneath her chin, he brought her gaze back to his. "It's just what?" he prompted.

Drawing a breath, she summoned the fortitude to confess her insecurities. "It's been a long time, Ford."

He seemed to consider that. "For us...or with any man?"

Certain she couldn't become any more embarrassed than she already was, she muttered, "Both."

He tilted his head, and smiled. "Would it help if I told you that it's been a long time for me, too?"

It did help, and there was enough honesty in his expression that she believed him.

"Tell you what, why don't we just start where we left off at the country club? We'll take this slow and easy, and we can put a halt to it anytime you want." The backs of his knuckles stroked her cheek, and gooseflesh rose on her skin. "You only need to tell me to stop and I will, okay?"

She nodded, appreciating that bit of security, and the right to change her mind at any time.

He indicated the bright lamp in the living room. "Can I turn off this light?"

"Yes," she said, preferring the softer illumination from the kitchen to guide them, instead of the harsh glare of the lamp. She watched him move away, and flip the switch on the wall, turning the room into an intimate, romantic setting. Then he came back to where she stood and stopped in front of her, and she could feel the heat of his muscular body, could smell the male scent of him.

"Would you mind if I took the clip from your hair? Or maybe you'd like to do it for me?" He made the suggestion lightly, but the husky quality to his voice was very revealing. "More than anything, I'd love to see your hair down."

He was giving her the choice, and she accepted it. Holding his watchful gaze, she reached up and unsnapped the clip securing the mass of hair on top of her head. Soft, buoyant curls cascaded to just below her shoulders, framing her face.

She thought she heard him suck in a breath, and her own heart skipped a beat. Silently, she willed him to touch her hair, and then he did, reverently threading his long fingers through the thick, warm strands.

A deep groan of pleasure rumbled from his throat. "It's still so rich, so silky," he said, awed. "Except I can see auburn highlights you never had before."

She felt oddly pleased that he noticed such a small detail. "It's gotten darker with age. As for the red, it must have come from my mother's side of the family."

He spent another minute luxuriating in the weight and texture of her hair, burying his hands in the mass and using his fingers to massage her scalp. Grace shivered and all but purred——his fascination with her hair was one of the more sensual experiences of her life.

"Can I kiss you now?"

She smiled up at him, feeling lethargic and complacent. "I'm not used to having someone ask permission to kiss me."

He grinned, too, stealing her breath with those gorgeous dimples. "I'm trying to be a gentleman, and give you that option to say stop."

She didn't want him to be chivalrous, not when she'd begun to ache deep inside for something more. Following her emotions, she said, "In that case, I'd like it very much if you kissed me."

He obliged her, taking time and care with her mouth, and slowly pulling her deeper into his embrace. She went willingly, sliding her hands over the hard contours of his chest, surrendering to the heat of his lips. His own palms caressed her leisurely. He cupped her breast gently through the material of her dress, grazed his thumb over the hardened tip, and she moaned at the exquisite pleasure. Sweet, hot desire, unlike any she'd ever known, electrified her body.

Breaking the escalating kiss, he pressed his lips to her temple, holding her close. "You're trembling, Grace," he murmured, his own body taut and restrained, but unmistakably aroused. "Should I take that as a good sign, or bad?"

She closed her eyes, and considered his question—another chance for her to change her mind. Nothing had ever felt as good or right as this moment. What had begun as tension had blossomed into quivering anticipation, and a need that transcended the mere act of making love. There was an emotional connection still between them, and it pulled at her heartstrings.

"Oh, it's a good sign," she reassured him, a bit of humor lacing her voice. Glancing up, she met his smoky gaze, and remembering her vow to please herself, she catered to the yearning deep within her. "Would you like to go into my bedroom?"

His breath seemed to leave him in a quiet rush. "Yeah, I'd like that."

Silently, she led him to her room, stopping at the side of her four-poster bed, covered in the mauve-and-blue quilt her mother had made for her when she'd turned sixteen. It was a cherished heirloom, one she'd hoped to pass on to her own daughter one day.

Refusing to think about lost dreams, she reached for the loosened tie around Ford's neck and disposed of it. Her hands went to his shirt, unbuttoning it with sure and steady fingers. Together, they worked to remove their clothing, which became a slow, seductive process of discovery that heightened the hunger and passion spiraling between them.

Time lost meaning, and the night turned magical. Ford spent an immeasurable amount of time acquainting himself with the womanly changes to her body, worshiping the supple, pliant curves she'd developed with his slow hands and generous mouth. In turn, she reveled in the impressive man he'd become, with well-formed muscles, and sleek, hot skin.

When he gently laid her on the bed and moved over her, her own flesh caught fire. Brushing the curls from her face, he kissed her, long and lazily. Finally, he lifted his head, and stared down at her with eyes filled with a combination of anguish and joy.

The poignant mixture of emotions made Grace's breath hitch in her chest.

"Ah, Grace, I really have missed you," he murmured, his voice low and deep and intimate.

She swallowed back the tightness in her throat and skimmed her fingers along his cheek. "Me, too."

His expression softened. A tender smile touched his mouth, relaxing the taut line of his jaw. With one arm bracing his heavy weight above her, his other hand continued to explore, shaping the swell of her breast, stroking over her hip, and finally parting her slender thighs to fit himself more fully against her.

She sighed, then gasped when his fingers brushed

along the juncture of her thighs. She arched toward him, moaning softly.

Her uninhibited response seemed to gratify him. Immensely. But he held his own desire in check, an uncertain frown marring his brow. "I've dreamed of this, of you, for so long. I want it to be perfect."

The glimpse of vulnerability reminded her of the boy he'd once been and made her realize that for as much as he'd gained wealth and confidence, some things hadn't changed at all.

"It will be," she told him, and drew his mouth to hers.

And it was. The pleasure he gave her was exquisite. Their loving became a meeting of lost souls, and a rejoicing of spirit.

And not once during the long, wonderful night did she tell him to stop.

Bam, bam, bam.

The pounding sound reverberating in Grace's mind grew louder, the voice calling her name more gruff and insistent. Ignoring the annoying noise, Grace snuggled closer to the warm, hard body curled against her from behind and willed the intruder away. Strong, male limbs entwined around her legs, and a corded arm banded possessively around her naked waist.

A sleepy smile curved her mouth. *Ford.* He was still there, testimony to the fact that their lovemaking hadn't been a fabulous, glorious dream. Floating somewhere between slumber and consciousness, she had the fleeting thought that maybe this time around things could be different for them. Maybe this time, they could find a way to be happy together.

The pounding continued. She frowned, and the man behind her stirred. A broad hand caressed her hip, and he buried his face in the crook of her neck. His voice was sleep-roughened when he murmured into her ear, "Grace, honey, someone is at your door."

Grace's eyes popped open at the same time her heart sped into overdrive. Surely, Ford was mistaken...no, sure enough, that obnoxious sound was coming from the front of her house.

Untangling herself from him and the covers, she stumbled out of bed, grabbed her robe from the connecting bathroom, and thrust her hands inside the sleeves, her disoriented mind whirring with a hundred thoughts. Mainly, who in the world could be here?

One glance at her reflection in the bathroom mirror made her cringe—she glowed, no doubt, but she looked like a tousled mess! Her hair tumbled around her face and shoulders in a wild disarray, her lips looked pink and swollen from Ford's ardent kisses, and there was even a red chafe mark on her neck. Since the person pummeling her front door sounded extremely persistent, not to mention impatient, she had no time to make herself presentable.

She passed through the bedroom, her gaze pausing briefly on the gorgeous man sprawled on his back on her bed. The covers swathed around his hips, leaving his chest gloriously bare. A sexy, lazy smile canted the corners of his mouth.

Ignoring the renewed awareness tickling her belly, she tightened the sash of her robe. "Stay in here," she ordered in a hushed voice.

"Don't worry, Grace," he murmured huskily. "I'll be here when you get back."

The invitation in his hazy violet eyes was clear, and her breasts tightened at the thought of spending a lazy Sunday morning in bed with Ford—just as soon as she got rid of her unexpected visitor.

The incessant knocking spurred her into action. Exiting the bedroom, she closed the door behind her, which put her right in the living room. "I'll be right there," she called in an attempt to inform the other person she was on her way.

Seeing Ford's suit jacket on her sofa, she stuffed the masculine article of clothing into the coat closet. With her still sleepy head struggling for wide-awake cognizance, she unlocked her front door, opened it...and came fully alert when she encountered her father standing on her porch, his face red with outrage.

"Dad," she said in a voice that was so tight it squeaked. "What are you doing here?"

He didn't answer her question, but barged past her and into her cottage without an invitation. Her father wasn't a tall man, but what he lacked in height he more than made up for in a physically fit body and sheer stubbornness. It was that headstrong will that sent a ripple of alarm through Grace.

His gold/brown gaze took in her disheveled appearance, and a scowl of disapproval darkened his expression. "It's after ten in the morning, Grace. What are you still doing in bed?"

Enjoying myself. Pleasing myself. Falling in love all over again. Biting back the private comments, she casually clutched her robe at her neck, too aware of the fact that she was naked beneath. Too aware, too, that her father was too close to her bedroom door for comfort. "It's Sunday, Dad," she said, heading into the kitchen, knowing he'd follow. "I don't have to work, so I can be as lazy as I want to be, which means sleeping in till noon, if I'd like."

"Hrmph." The sound of disgust erupted from somewhere behind Grace—a typical sound from her father. Ellis Holbrook believed in rising early and making the most of a day. Grace did, too, but she'd wanted to make the most of her day with Ford. Especially since he was leaving today. They had things to discuss, like what they were going to do about their new relationship, and how they were going to make a long-distance romance work between them.

Filling her coffee carafe with water, she glanced over her shoulder at her dad. "Why didn't you call before coming out here like you normally do?"

"What, I'm not allowed to stop by and see my daughter any time I want?"

Refusing to give into his guilt tactics, she smiled at him sweetly as she scooped coffee grounds into the basket. "I'm just surprised to see you, is all. Didn't you go golfing this morning with Gene and Emmett?" Rain or shine, her father had a standing reservation with his two old friends to play eighteen holes at the Whitaker Country Club on Sunday mornings. Only a medical emergency or some other life-threatening crisis could drag him away from the sport—which was what worried Grace.

"I was golfing, when we came across Sheldon and his golfing buddies out on the ninth hole. He imparted some disturbing news that ruined my game."

Sheldon was the president of the only savings and loan in town. Suspecting where this conversation might be headed, she remained nonchalant. "Oh, and what news was that?"

"Ford McCabe is back in town." Ellis's face flushed again, a long-ago rage brewing just below the surface.

Grace's stomach clenched tight, and she tried desperately to act surprised at his announcement. "Sheldon saw him?"

"No, he didn't see him." He scrubbed a hand through his thick, salt-and-pepper hair, the gesture agitated. Her father normally had calm, steady nerves, but not where Ford McCabe was concerned. "Yesterday after closing time at the bank Sheldon was reviewing the new accounts and came across a savings and checking account under the name of Ford McCabe. The signature card was signed with Ford's name and dated yesterday."

Grace wasn't sure what to make of that, and wondered why Ford hadn't told her anything about the bank account last night. Certain there was a logical explanation for the information her father had discovered, she shook off the unease settling over her, and turned toward the cupboard to retrieve two coffee cups.

Her father paced the small confines of the kitchen, the volatile energy surrounding him nearly palpable. "And guess what *company* is listed under his place of business?" He didn't give her time to guess the answer to his question, though her belly twisted with an awful apprehension. "FZM, Inc. He's the owner of the company who bought the land out at Cutter

Creek! That house is listed as his primary residence!''

Ford was going to be *living* in Whitaker Falls? Why hadn't he told her? Grace's mind reeled, and a horrible sense of betrayal pierced her heart. The hand pouring the coffee into their mugs shook uncontrollably, and she set the pot back on the burner before she spilled hot liquid everywhere.

With her mind and body numb from disbelief, and a dozen other different emotions clamoring to the surface, Grace brought their mugs to the table. She sat through a cup of coffee with her father while he groused about Ford McCabe and spilled the bitter emotions that had accumulated in the aftermath of Ford's departure eleven years ago.

Grace made the appropriate comments she knew her father wanted to hear, but all she could think about was confronting the naked man in her bed once her father left. After what she'd shared with Ford last night, she felt confused, and deceived by his omission.

She didn't offer her father a refill on his coffee, and instead told him she had errands to run and things to do. She walked him to the door, and he stopped just as they entered the living room, staring at all the vases of roses. He appeared perplexed—in his upset state, he obviously hadn't noticed them upon his arrival.

''What's with all the roses?'' he asked.

Grace grasped for the most logical excuse. ''Excess inventory from the shop, so I thought I'd bring them home to enjoy.''

Melancholy touched Ellis Holbrook's expression as he breathed deeply of an arrangement of roses.

"I still miss her, you know," he said, and Grace knew he was talking about her mother, Felice. "But if she were here, I know she'd be very proud of you and your flower shop."

Grace placed a gentle hand on her father's back as they walked to the door. "Yeah, I know she would be."

Ellis stepped out onto the porch and turned toward her, his sentimental expression hardening with resolve, and his eyes firing with purpose, as if he'd suddenly remembered his reason for coming out to her cottage. "I'm warning you, Grace, if that no-good McCabe boy comes around, stay away from him! He was nothing but trouble eleven years ago, and he's nothing but trouble now."

She refrained from informing her father that Ford was no longer a boy, but a splendidly grown man. "Maybe he's changed," she said, though she was beginning to doubt that herself after what she'd just learned.

Her father scoffed at that. "You've always had a soft heart, Grace, but maybe you should keep in mind that Ford McCabe killed Aaron and destroyed our family, not to mention what he did to *you*." Hostility and resentment dripped from his tone.

Grace inwardly winced, knowing that Ford could hear her conversation with her father. Someone had seen her and Ford together eleven years ago, and after the tragic death of her brother rumor of her involvement with Ford had spread, and ultimately cast a shadow over her reputation. Her father blamed Ford for that as well, of course, even though she'd been a willing party to what had happened back then. It was just easier for her father to believe Ford was responsible for ruining her virtue than accept that she'd consented to the relationship.

"Whatever reason he's decided to come back to live in Whitaker Falls, it can't be good," her father said tightly. "Stay away from him."

On that heated note, her father was gone.

Shutting the door, Grace leaned against the flat surface and closed her eyes, her heart aching in her chest.

"Is it safe to come out?"

Startled by the deep voice, Grace lifted her head, and found Ford standing in the doorway to her bedroom, his shoulder leaning negligently against the jamb. He was no longer naked, thank goodness. He'd put his slacks and shirt back on, looking nothing like the sensual, affectionate man she'd left in bed twenty minutes ago. No, now there was a dark, ruthless quality to him that made her realize just how little she knew about the man he'd become.

When she didn't say anything, he pushed off the doorjamb and strolled into the living room toward her, his expression unreadable. "I guess your father's feelings toward me are one of the things that haven't changed since I've been gone."

She choked on a humorless laugh. "You're right about that," she confirmed, moving toward the sofa as he closed the distance between them. Last night, she'd trusted Ford, with her heart and her body. This morning, she felt disillusioned and uncertain of his motives. "What *business* brings you here, Ford?" she asked, giving him one last chance to make amends.

He stopped in the middle of the room, his entire

demeanor tensing. Shadows clouded his gaze, concealing truths, and her heart wrenched painfully.

"No more lies, Ford," she whispered around the ache in her throat. "I know about the house out at Cutter Creek being yours. My father found out from Sheldon at the bank. You're FZM, Inc."

He released a deep, harsh breath and scrubbed a hand over his stubbled jaw. After a long, strained moment, he said, "Yes, I'm FZM, Inc, which stands for Ford Zachariah McCabe. The house out at Cutter Creek is mine, and I'm here to give the house one final walk-through before the carpet and tile are installed and the furniture delivered. In about five weeks, I'm moving in."

She stared at him, the hurt and devastation coursing through her excruciating in its intensity. "You *lied*."

A muscle in his cheek ticked, his eyes turning dark and unfathomable. "I hadn't meant for you to find out this way."

That was it, just a flat, emotionless excuse that made a mockery of their night together. He offered no other explanation, and what pride she still had left kept her from demanding a more credible answer.

Tears burned the back of her eyes, but she valiantly blinked them back. She'd hoped this time around would be different for them, but she no longer trusted his intentions, or his purpose for returning. She couldn't even be sure what they'd shared last night had been real for him.

Lifting her chin, she clung desperately to what little was left of her composure. "I think it would be best if I took you back to the Hampton Inn."

He didn't argue or object. Didn't attempt to deny her request. It was as though he'd closed himself off to her emotionally. Instead he nodded curtly, a virtual stranger, then turned to retrieve the rest of his things from her bedroom, leaving Grace to endure the same heartbreaking loss she'd experienced when he'd left her eleven years ago.

Except this time, her grief was tinged with Ford's deceit.

CHAPTER FOUR

"THAT nasty flu bug still hasn't gone away?"

Grace glanced up as Dr. Randal Chase walked into the examination room of the medical office he shared with her father, her medical chart in hand. "Unfortunately, no." She gave him a smile as wan as her body and spirit felt. "The nausea seems to come and go in waves. It's strange, really. One moment I feel fine, and then the next I feel like I'm going to lose what's in my stomach. I've been light-headed as well, and my body feels achy."

He adjusted the gold wire-rimmed glasses on the bridge of his nose and offered a warm, sympathetic smile. "While I do a quick, routine examine, I'll have Marcie pull your lab report to see what the tests we did a few days ago reveal. Hop up onto the examination table."

Grace did as he ordered, sitting on the edge of the narrow table covered in a thin layer of tissue paper. Setting her chart on a nearby counter, he poked his head out the door, gave Marcie instructions to bring him Grace's lab report, and returned to his patient. Using his stethoscope, he listened to her heart and lungs, proclaiming everything clear and in order.

"Stick out your tongue and say *ahhh,*" he said, withdrawing a tiny flashlight from his white lab coat pocket. Flattening her tongue with a wooden depressor, he checked her throat and tonsils. "Everything looks fine. Lie down on the table and I'll check your stomach."

Marcie delivered the requested report, setting it on the counter, then disappeared again. Grace reclined back on the stiff table, and the doctor slipped his hands beneath her blouse to continue his examination. "Have you been feeling bloated?"

"A little," she confessed, then sucked in a breath when his chilled fingers touched her belly.

"Sorry 'bout that. My hands are a little cold today." His fingers moved efficiently and impersonally over her, probing gently. As he continued, he said absently, "I hear that furniture has been delivered to that monstrous house out at Cutter Creek."

Grace's stomach rolled at the mention of Ford's property, which was now common knowledge among the residents of Whitaker Falls. Closing her eyes, she swallowed the nausea rising in the back of her throat.

"Hmm," she replied noncommittally, suspecting his idle comment was an attempt to keep her mind on his verbal exchange, and not his exploring fingers. The vacant house at Cutter Creek was the hot topic of conversation in town, as was speculation of Ford McCabe's return.

Ford had been gone for almost five weeks, and she was beginning to wonder if maybe her fluctuating "flu" was possibly some kind of stress disorder. She dreaded his return, thought about it constantly, and agonized incessantly over the fact that he'd deceived her. His duplicity was never far from her mind, nor was her own gullibility—without a doubt, she'd been a fool to fall back into his arms so easily. Considering she hadn't heard from Ford since he'd left, she'd concluded that their night together hadn't meant as much to him as it had her.

She groaned when Dr. Chase poked at a particularly tender area near her uterus.

He frowned, his touch lightening. "Am I hurting you?"

"It's just a little uncomfortable," she acknowledged.

He motioned for her to sit up, and made a few notations on her chart, his back to her. "Marcie said she saw a champagne-colored sports coupe heading down the gravel driveway toward the house this morning on her way to work. It seems your father's nemesis has returned."

Ford was back!

Grace pressed her fingers to her temple in an attempt to stop the spinning in her head—from sitting up too fast or that last bit of unsettling news, she wasn't sure. Even after four and a half weeks, she still hadn't come to terms with the fact that Ford McCabe would be living in Whitaker Falls permanently.

Dr. Chase turned back toward her, his demeanor turning professional once again. "Physically, everything seems in order." He opened the file with her test results. "Let's see about your lab report." His index finger skimmed down the page. "Your thyroid looks good, blood sugar is fine, cholesterol is right where it should be..." His finger stopped and he glanced up at her, undisguised surprise in his eyes. "This says you're pregnant."

"You tested for pregnancy?"

He shrugged. "Just trying to rule out all probable

causes for your symptoms. According to this, you're positive.''

Her mouth suddenly felt dry as cotton. ''That's impossible. I'm sterile.''

''Says who?''

''David and I...we couldn't have children. He's gone on to have two kids, so that leaves me.''

''That doesn't mean anything.'' He regarded her with kind blue eyes. ''Were you ever tested for infertility?''

''No...'' The admission came reluctantly.

He contemplated her reply for a moment, then grabbed her chart again. ''When was your last menstrual period?'' He clicked his ballpoint pen, poised to jot down the information.

''I'm not very regular, so I don't keep track.'' She'd never had a reason to mark her calendar and count days because she was inevitably late. ''I'd say somewhere around six weeks ago. I should start any day.''

Seemingly taking her comment face value—that she hadn't been sexually active as of late—he made a note about her irregular cycle then met her gaze through his wire-rimmed glasses. ''It sounds like a false positive to me, or an error at the lab.''

She pasted on a bright, agreeable smile. ''I'm sure you're right.''

''And then there's always the possibility of immaculate conception,'' he said with a playful wink.

She laughed, but the light sound did nothing to ease the pounding of her heart, or the thought that kept popping into her head. *Could she really be pregnant?* She mentally scanned through her symptoms, and though she'd never been pregnant before, what she was experiencing were classic signs as she'd heard other women describe them.

How could that be possible? Had she and David just been incompatible in as that they hadn't been able to conceive a child together? Questions bombarded her mind, but as much as she wanted answers, she refused to ask Dr. Chase and risk his suspicion.

"Why don't you stay home for the next few days to rest and have Dora run the shop?" he suggested. "If you're not feeling better by Monday, then come in and see me again."

She nodded, feeling numb, confused, and more out of sorts than when she'd first arrived. Grabbing her purse, she stopped Dr. Chase before they exited the examination room. "I'd like to exercise my doctor patient privilege and keep this between you and me," she said, stating her preference that her father not discover the results of that lab test.

"All right," Dr. Chase said slowly, digesting her request and coming to his own conclusions. He hesitated for a moment, then his gaze softened. "Just because you and David couldn't get pregnant doesn't mean you're sterile, Grace. There are a lot of variables when it comes to reasons why a couple can't conceive, and even if you were tested and confirmed as infertile, there is always that miracle of a chance that you could still get pregnant and have a family."

Grace nodded, unable to bring herself to tell Dr. Chase that although that bit of news thrilled her, it also struck an awful fear in her heart because she suspected her irresponsible actions with Ford might have produced irrevocable consequences.

* * *

Ford's fingers tensed on the steering wheel of his car as he turned down Oakton Avenue and headed toward Whitaker Town Square. Nearly five weeks after making love with Grace, Ford still couldn't shake the regret that had lodged itself deep within him...regret for the way he'd handled the situation, and for hurting Grace with his stubborn silence.

And then there was also the heavy dose of guilt that had played tug-of-war with his conscience over the ensuing weeks. He should have told her the truth about Cutter Creek and FZM that night at dinner, but he'd believed he had time on his side to sway her, to court her, to gradually prove to her that he'd changed and belonged in her world.

Her father had stolen that opportunity from him, had reduced his plans to ashes with his harsh words and the bitter blame Ellis had cast upon him. From Grace's bedroom, Ford had heard Ellis's ranting, his dredging up of the ugly past, the accusations that had haunted him since the day Aaron had died. In that moment, all the years Ford had spent rebuilding his life and developing credibility had been crushed into insignificance by one man's hatred.

Old doubts and insecurities had settled in, mocking him with the possibility that he'd never be good enough for Grace Holbrook. He'd retreated when Grace had confronted him, a self-preservation tactic he'd learned as an impoverished kid, to protect himself from all the criticism he'd had to endure. It seemed his instincts were just as sharp now.

She'd been angry that morning; he'd been defensive after listening to Ellis malign his character. Leaving seemed the best thing to do to let their tempers cool, to allow Grace time to absorb the fact that he'd be living in Whitaker Falls. Permanently. He had a reputation to establish, and his pride to win back.

In time, he would earn both.

But for now, it was time to find out if Grace's reception would be any warmer than that of the few locals he'd encountered who'd eyed him with cool reserve.

She was pregnant. Without a doubt. The bright blue strip on the home pregnancy test Grace had bought at the drugstore, along with the twenty other inconsequential items she'd purchased in an attempt to camouflage the glaring evidence, confirmed the lab results had been accurate. With a deep, internal shudder, Grace lowered herself to the closed lid of the commode and squeezed her eyes shut in an attempt to suppress the tears burning the back of her throat.

She lost the battle, the rush of moisture seeping past her lashes. One blink, and a tear rolled down her cheek, then another. Oh, what a fine mess she'd gotten herself into!

She pressed a hand to her still-flat tummy, guessing in another month or two her secret would be revealed to anyone who glanced her way. While she was ecstatic that she was able to have babies, she dreaded the emotional battle that lay ahead for her and her child, not to mention the possible scandal. Not only would she remain unwed in her pregnant condition, but not naming a father would surely add to the ensuing speculation. There was no way she was going to compound her mistake by announcing to everyone that Ford was the daddy.

She'd tell Ford her intentions up-front—that she planned to have this baby on her own, and wanted absolutely nothing from him except his silence. Since he obviously didn't love her, and had his own personal agenda for returning to Whitaker Falls, she was certain she'd be able to gain his cooperation.

As for her father...well, she wondered if he'd believe Dr. Chase's suggestion of immaculate conception.

Releasing a shuddering sigh, she managed a wobbly smile for the unexpected gift she'd been blessed with. She wasn't one to wallow in misery and mistakes, and she refused to do so with this situation. This child would know love...*her* love, and that's all that mattered.

A knock on her front door startled Grace, and kicked her heart rate into triple-time. Her mind spun as she took in the contents of the pregnancy test spread out on the bathroom counter. Guessing the uninvited guest was her father, who'd made a habit of dropping by on impulse lately, Grace frantically cleaned up the incriminating evidence. She shoved the small plastic cup and the instruction booklet into the box they came in and tossed it into the cupboard beneath the sink.

Another knock.

Swiping at her damp eyes with the heel of her hand, and trying to calm the jumble of nerves fluttering in her belly, she made her way through the living room. She opened the front door with a smile she'd dredged up from her cheerful reserve, which promptly fell into a frown when she found Ford standing on her porch.

Gone was the executive who'd seduced her,

traded in for more casual attire that suited him just as well as the expensive wardrobe from his first visit. A pale blue striped Western shirt covered his wide, athletic chest, the threads of color making his violet eyes more dazzling, and intense. Crisp, new, form-fitting blue jeans hugged a lean waist and hips, and outlined nice firm thighs. Leather cowboy boots completed the ensemble. He still looked successful, and incredibly gorgeous. And he still had the ability to set her pulse to racing—damn him.

"Hi." Though his voice was rich, intimate, and just as sexy as she remembered, his eyes were dark and reserved. "I stopped by your flower shop, but Dora said you'd gone home sick. You do look pale, and your eyes are puffy. Are you okay?"

His gaze scrutinized her face with a gentle concern Grace refused to believe was real. "I'm fine." Her lips pursed in irritation. It was one thing knowing he was living in Whitaker Falls and having to deal with the possibility of seeing him in town, but it was another for him to think he could drop by her place uninvited. "What are you doing here?"

Her demand didn't seem to faze him. "Considering where we left off last time, I think we have unfinished business to take care of. I gave you time to cool off, so the sooner we get this conversation over with, the better."

She opted for a short and simple response. "I have nothing to say to you, so leave."

Anticipating her next move, he wedged his booted foot into the jamb, effectively stopping the door from shutting in his face. His large hand clamped around the frame, and she knew it wouldn't take much effort for him to push his way into her cottage.

"I'm not leaving until we talk, Grace." He sounded firm and too determined.

"Then talk," she said through the three-inch of space separating them.

"Without the door between us." Annoyance touched his deep voice.

Suspecting Ford possessed a tenacity to match all that self-assurance he'd developed over the years, she reluctantly let him into her living room. Closing the door, she headed toward the kitchen, needing something cool to drink to offset the heat prickling along her skin.

He followed, watching her as she retrieved a tall glass from the cupboard and filled it with iced tea from the refrigerator. "I'm waiting," she said impatiently.

Coming up beside her, he grabbed his own glass and took the pitcher from her before she could put it away, pouring himself his own drink. She frowned at him, but he ignored her as he drained the liquid, then refilled his glass a second time.

He leaned a hip against the tiled kitchen counter, looking thoroughly masculine and as though he belonged in her cottage. His gaze swept over her, slow and searching. "So what's this about you not feeling well?"

She wasn't mentally or emotionally ready to spring the truth on him, not when she hadn't yet had a chance to get used to the reality of her being pregnant. "I've had the flu, so don't get too close." She curled the corner of her lip, daring him to ignore her warning so she could take great pleasure in infecting him—if only her illness *was* contagious!

He laughed, low and husky. "You should know

by now that I'm not afraid to swap germs with you."

His confidence astounded her, and worried her. Something in her stomach unfurled—not a bout of nausea, but a sensual rippling of awareness she couldn't restrain. Was she forever doomed to be attracted to this man despite everything he'd done to deceive her?

When it became clear that she wasn't going to take his bait, he set his empty glass next to the sink, growing serious. "I was really hoping the past few weeks would have made you see a little bit of reason."

She gaped at him. "How can I reason the fact that you deceived me?"

Regret clouded his handsome features. "I omitted a few things, true—"

"Just the teensy-weensy fact that the huge, sprawling house out at Cutter Creek is yours, and you'll be living in Whitaker Falls." She snapped her fingers, as if remembering a few more points. "Oh, not to mention that you're wealthy, successful and you own your own company now."

His jaw hardened, and he pushed his fingers through his thick hair in a frustrated gesture, saying nothing. His expression grew hard, impenetrable, defensive.

Grace took a drink of her tea, trying to calm the riot of confusion weaving through her. What they'd shared a month ago had been honest and real on her part, but she didn't know what to believe of Ford's intentions, could only remember his lies, and that awful sense of betrayal she'd felt upon learning the truth of *who* he was now. She couldn't help but ponder what else he might be hiding behind that reserved expression of his.

Taking a deep breath, she asked, "Does anyone besides me know you're back in town?"

He shrugged those broad shoulders of his. "I've run into a few people. I'm not hiding the fact that I'm back, considering I'm going to be a permanent part of the community."

She dragged a hand through her disheveled hair, feeling weary to the bone. "Yeah, well, the residents here have a long memory, so if you're expecting a parade in honor of your return, don't hold your breath."

A pained look passed over his features. "I know full well what most everyone thinks of me, and I'm hoping their opinions will change in time. I'm not the wild, rebellious kid I was when I left. What I've done, what I've become, has to count for something."

She thought she detected the barest hint of hope in his voice, saw the briefest glimpse of the lonely boy he'd been—a scrappy kid who'd wanted nothing more but to be welcomed and accepted by the town he'd grown up in. Steeling herself against the urge to fall for such a convincing, heartfelt act, she thought of her father and what *his* reaction would be. "My father blames you for Aaron's death. I doubt *his* opinion will change anytime soon."

Though he leaned negligently against the counter, his body screamed with tension. His gaze clung to hers, as if needing an anchor from the condemnation he was sure to face from Ellis Holbrook. "Do *you* blame me?"

She felt the silent pull of his question on her heart,

her conscience. He wanted, *needed,* to hear that she didn't hold him responsible for her brother's tragic death. As much as she ached to say the words, she knew she'd be a fool to fall for his plea and give him that leverage over her emotions, not when she now had something much more emotional at stake— her baby.

"It doesn't matter what I think," she said in the most impassive tone of voice she could manage.

The vulnerable, lost little boy look in his eyes evaporated, hardening into resolve. Releasing a sigh filled with disgust, he pushed off the counter and brushed past her, leaving the kitchen. Grace moved to the window above the sink and closed her eyes, swallowing the huge lump that had gathered in her throat.

Relief, and an odd sense of disappointment coursed through her as she waited to hear Ford leave. But instead of the front door opening, she heard the bathroom door close—no doubt he was emptying his bladder after gulping two glasses of iced tea.

A minute later, she heard him exit the bathroom and sent a fervent prayer that he'd leave now. They certainly had nothing left to say to each other.

Her wish wasn't to be.

"What is this?" Ford asked from behind her.

Turning around at the curious tone of his voice, her eyes widened in alarm when she saw what had prompted his question. "Give me that!" she demanded, attempting to grab the plastic stick from his fingers.

He effortlessly held it out of her reach. "Isn't this one of those home pregnancy test things?"

Her stomach clenched, and anger burned through her like acid. "You had no right to go snooping through my personal things!"

"Snooping?" His brows rose indignantly at the insult. "It was sitting right next to the bathroom sink!"

Surely she wouldn't have been so careless. "It was not!" she said through clenched teeth.

"Was so," he argued mildly, though there was nothing calm about the stormy shade of his eyes. "Maybe you were in a big hurry when you heard someone knock on the door and you overlooked hiding it."

That gave her a moment's pause to think about her frantic actions when she'd stuffed everything into the box. Good, Lord, she honestly couldn't remember putting the plastic strip in there as well. "Regardless, it's none of your business." She lunged for the incriminating evidence again, only for him to smoothly intercept her efforts.

Holding the plastic strip out of her proximity, he eyed it critically. "The way I see things, it's very much my business if this blue strip means you're pregnant." His brows pulled into a perplexed frown as he looked at her. "Although that confuses the hell out of me since you told me you couldn't get pregnant."

Crossing her arms over her achy, tender breasts, she lifted her chin mutinously, refusing to answer or explain anything to him.

Ford waited for Grace to confirm or deny his statement, but came to the conclusion that nothing was going to slip past those tight lips, or that obstinate attitude of hers. His gaze slid down the length of her in a slow, deliberate search for clues, but the loose blouse and gauzy skirt she wore offered no help in determining her condition. He saw no real evidence to confirm the test he held in his hands—the one Grace was so anxious to steal back.

Frustrated with her stubbornness, he decided it was time she learned what a formidable opponent he could be when it came to a battle of wills. "All I have to do is take this to the drugstore and ask the clerk which test it came from and read the instructions on the box to find out whether or not this little blue strip means positive or negative. I'm sure that would set some tongues to wagging, not to mention gossip flying. And then it would only be a matter of a month or two before rumor *blossoms* into fact," he added meaningfully.

Her gaze narrowed on him, loathing sparking the gold in her eyes. "You're wretched, you know that?"

"Wretched?" He raised a brow at her unflattering description. "I have every right to know the truth."

She huffed in exasperation, her full breasts rising and falling with the gesture. "I don't know why you'd even care what that blue strip means!"

His brows snapped together in offense. "Of course I care."

"Why?" A suspicious moisture shimmered in her eyes. "You made me no promises before we slept together."

He didn't think it possible, but his heart hurt. "Grace..." He stepped toward her, but when she backed away, he stopped. "You can't believe I'd ever disregard something so important."

"You lied and deceived me," she pointed out, her

voice wavering with emotion. "Of course I can believe you're capable of just about anything."

Sighing, he scrubbed a hand down his face, belatedly realizing his mistake in keeping Grace in the dark about his return. "I never meant to hurt you, Grace. That's something you're just going to have to believe."

"I don't know if I *can* trust you." Her shoulders slumped in defeat, and her gaze dropped to the plastic stick that had caused so much contention. "Yes, it's a pregnancy test," she confessed quietly. "And the blue strip means it's positive. The doctor confirmed it as well."

Feeling as though someone had pulled the rug right out from under him, Ford lowered himself to one of the chairs at the small oak table in the kitchen. He stared at the blue strip in bewilderment. "What happened to you not being able to get pregnant?"

"Consider yourself exceptionally virile." Her tone was droll.

He glanced up, his mouth quirking with a smile. "I suppose that's good to know, but I have to admit this is quite a surprise."

"No doubt," she said bitterly. "Don't worry, Ford, I don't want or expect anything from you, except your silence that you're the baby's father."

Seeing the determined look on her face, a cold, hard knot formed in his stomach. "What the hell is that supposed to mean?"

That chin of hers lifted. "I'm keeping *my* baby—"

He stood, approaching her. "Of course you're keeping *my* baby—"

She stepped back, her hand resting protectively on her still-flat tummy. "I'm raising *my* baby on *my* own—"

He closed the distance between them, until he had her cornered between him, and the counter. "I'll be damned if I let you raise *my* baby on your own."

She went on as if she hadn't heard him, though the touch of nervousness in her gaze spoke volumes. "And it would make things much simpler if you just relinquished all rights as *my* baby's father."

Fury boiled within him. "I'll just bet it would," he said in a dangerously low voice. Did she think he was such a monster that he'd abandon his own child and willing give up his parental rights? Well, she was about to learn exactly what a villain he could be. For him, there was only one solution to their predicament. An *unnegotiable* one. One she'd surely oppose.

"We're getting married," he stated.

She gasped in outrage. "This is the modern world, McCabe, and I don't have to do any such thing!" She followed that up with a jab to his chest with her index finger. "The last thing I want is to marry you. *My* baby and I are better off on our own."

"*Our* baby," he said through gritted teeth, though his attempt at a compromise made little difference in her eyes. Did she even remember that he'd been an integral part of creating that baby she carried?

She tried to inch around him, but he wasn't about to let her escape on the last word. He had too much to lose. Bracing his hands on either side of her on the counter, he trapped her within his arms. She instantly looked peeved at his tactic, but he didn't care.

"Dammit, Grace, quit being so unreasonable. You live in a small town, the people of which have narrow-minded views on illegitimate pregnancies. I believe that fits under the heading of one of those things that *hasn't* changed around here."

"I'm a big girl, Ford. Not only can I take care of myself, I'm prepared to handle the trials of being an unwed mother."

"Well, I refuse to allow my child to grow up with the stigma of being illegitimate," he said adamantly. "Did you think about the repercussions of *that*, Grace?"

He could see by her startled expression that she hadn't.

Old, bitter memories reared their ugly head, making him more determined to legitimize the child Grace carried. "I'm sorry to ruin your plans, but I'm not keeping the parentage of *our* baby a secret. I want to be a part of this child's life, and I'll be damned if I'll shirk my responsibility to my son or daughter."

She looked unswayed, mulishly so. No, she didn't trust him at all.

He shifted his stance, but his arms remained banded on either side of her. "If we don't get married, *our* child will be ridiculed, an outcast, and suffer the consequences of *our* actions. I've been there, Grace. I've been illegitimate, and I *refuse* to allow that to happen to any child of mine."

She opened her mouth to reply, but he pressed his fingers over her soft lips, not wanting her to inter-

rupt, or argue. This was one debate she would not
win.

"So, I'm not giving you a choice in the matter,
not when it comes to *my* baby's welfare." Her expression turned stricken, tearing at his heart. Hating
the strife between them, he gently strummed his fingers along her cheek, gratified when she didn't
flinch or jerk away. "The last thing I'd ever want
to do is trap you in a marriage you don't want. But
no matter how you feel about me, think about that
innocent baby and what kind of life it would have
carrying the stigma of being illegitimate."

"I wouldn't allow that to happen." Her voice was
small, not nearly as confident as it should have been.

A sad smile touched his mouth. "Oh, you could
try and shelter our child from taunts and whispers
behind his or her back, but take it from someone
who has lived that hell firsthand—there's always
someone who isn't afraid to speak their mind, regardless of anyone else's feelings."

She swallowed and looked away, but not before
he'd glimpsed the confusion filling her luminous
brown eyes. She knew what he spoke of was the
truth, because she'd heard and witnessed the personal taunts cast his way as a youth. There were
people in Whitaker Falls who would respect Grace
and the child she carried because of her relation to
Dr. Ellis Holbrook, but there were others who would
express their cruel opinions without any thought to
who they hurt.

Ford moved away from Grace, giving her the
breathing room she seemed to need, but still kept
his gaze on her. "We're getting married, Grace, and
this baby will have my name and grow up with a

mother and father who will love him or her." His ultimatum was firm and indisputable. "I'll expect nothing less, so you might as well get used to the idea of being Mrs. Grace McCabe."

She kept her lips tightly compressed and said nothing—she obviously knew there was nothing she could say that would make him change his mind about them getting married. The baby she carried changed everything between them, and he wouldn't accept no for an answer.

"And because I'm such a nice guy, I'll give you a week to get used to the idea of being married to me," he said, suspecting she'd need those seven days to get her affairs in order, and to break the news to her father.

"How gracious," she muttered.

He remained ruthless. "I'll set up a private appointment with Reverend Jones for next Saturday at one. Invite whomever you'd like."

Her lips curled up at the corner in mockery. "I'll be there with bells on."

He ignored her sarcasm, but couldn't overlook the devious glint in her eyes. She was playing the complacent female for him right now, but he wasn't about to chance that she'd pull a stunt that would leave him standing at the altar without a bride. "If you decide not to show up, then I'll be putting an ad in the *Whitaker Falls Weekly* announcing the impending arrival of *our* baby so there's no mistaking whose child it is that you're carrying."

She glared, the slightest bit of hope he'd detected in her gaze dwindling to resolve. "You really are wretched."

CHAPTER FIVE

"WHAT are you doing here on your wedding day?" Dora chastised as Grace entered her shop the following Saturday morning.

"It's better than sitting at home," Grace replied, setting her purse on a clear spot on the workbench behind the counter. She offered Dora what she hoped came off as a cheerful smile, though she was feeling anything but. She'd had a horrible morning, and her plans for the afternoon certainly didn't offer much comfort. Her and Ford's "appointment" with Reverend Jones had her insides twisting with nerves. "The quiet is enough to drive me insane lately, and I'd rather keep myself busy here."

Dora nodded in sympathetic understanding, and clipped the stem of a yellow daisy before pushing it into the floral arrangement. Needing an outlet for Ford's ultimatum, Grace had confessed everything about her relationship with Ford to Dora, who'd become one of her best friends over the past few years. She'd shared her past with Ford, his secretive return, her unexpected pregnancy, and finally the news of her upcoming nuptials. Dora had been a sympathetic listener, which Grace had desperately needed a week ago when she'd been so confused and overwhelmed by everything.

She was still feeling confused and overwhelmed—especially after her tension-filled visit with her father that morning—but she was resigned to marrying Ford. The argument Ford had issued on his child's behalf was strong and solid, motivated by painful memories of his own upbringing. She and Ford might be at odds, but she couldn't fault him for insisting on doing the honorable thing and legitimizing his child.

What Grace found difficult to forgive was the fact that Ford had lied to her and deceived her that first night he'd returned—even if only for the purpose of being "cautious" in his approach. She'd trusted him, had surrendered to emotions and needs and made love with him, and he'd betrayed her with half-truths. His deception made her wonder what else he might be hiding, and that disturbing thought made her realize how little she knew about the man Ford had become, and how the past eleven years had shaped him.

Not wanting to dwell on any other secrets her husband-to-be might be harboring, she picked up an invoice from the wooden table and perused the order for a Cheer Me Up bouquet to be sent to Mrs. Lord, who'd broken her leg two days ago.

"What time is Ford supposed to pick you up?" Dora asked, casting her a curious look.

"He'll be at my house at twelve-thirty, so I'll head back around twelve." That had been the extent of her conversation with Ford the past week—a brief phone call to confirm the time of the appointment with Reverend Jones, and when Ford would be at her cottage to pick her up. Glancing at her gold wristwatch, she noted the time, figuring that gave her another hour to try to relax her churning stomach.

Dora headed toward the glass enclosed refrigerating unit. "Well, since you're here, it saves me from having to drive out to your place for a delivery.''

Grace watched Dora return with two square floral boxes, and frowned. ''To deliver what?''

Her friend grinned enthusiastically. ''These.''

Grace stared in stunned surprise at the two items Dora produced from the boxes. One was a lovely crown of pink roses with baby's breath, and the other was a lush, gorgeous nosegay of the same design. Thin, streaming ribbons of pale pink and white matched the outfit she'd told Dora she'd be wearing today for her wedding when her assistant had casually asked a few days ago. She'd decided on a simple pink linen skirt and matching jacket with a white silk blouse, and the headdress and bouquet Dora had made complemented the colors perfectly.

She lightly fingered the soft petal of a rose and breathed in the delicate fragrance of the fresh flowers, touched by the sweet gesture. ''Oh, Dora, you shouldn't have.''

''Oh, I didn't.'' A wry smile canted Dora's mouth. ''Your *fiancé* came in earlier this week and ordered them. He asked me to find out what you'd be wearing, and to make sure the pieces matched.''

Grace's breath caught, and she silently damned Ford for being so thoughtful and wreaking additional havoc on her already jumbled emotions. She didn't want him to be nice and sweet, which only served to chip away at her resolve to keep her feelings out of the marriage she'd agreed to. They were marrying for practical reasons, for their baby's sake, and she had to keep that important fact foremost in her mind.

''You know,'' Dora began thoughtfully, capturing Grace's attention. ''For all the gossip I've been hearing this week about Ford McCabe and what a hooligan he supposedly is, I just don't see it myself. He comes across as very respectable, quite the gentleman, and gorgeous to boot."

"You weren't around when he was a hell-raiser of the worst sort and causing trouble for everyone." She absently curled a finger around the satiny ribbon from the nosegay, fearing her heartstrings would become just as ensnared by Ford's charm and romantic persuasion if she wasn't careful. She glanced back at Dora, who waited to hear more. " 'Respectable' is the last word anyone in Whitaker Falls would use to describe Ford. When he was a teenager he stole regularly from the Cash and Carry market, went joyriding in George Godwin's rebuilt '57 Chevy and wrecked it, set fire to Ken Olsen's barn and nearly killed one of his prized quarter horses, and though he was never caught, everyone assumes he's the one who busted in the windows of the After Hours bar and did over ten thousand dollars worth of damage to the place."

Grace ticked each transgression off on her fingers, but her mind lingered on that last misdeed. She'd made the same assumption as everyone else about the break-in at After Hours. Ford had had a personal vendetta against the bar where his mother worked and spent her paychecks on booze, and practically lived her life, so it hadn't been difficult to deduct who the culprit had been. After Hours had since become a run-down, shady bar that catered to a more unsavory clientele, hurting the other respectable establishments in that same strip of shops and businesses. The shop tenants were hoping the new property owner of the buildings, who had yet to be named, would do something to restore order to the shoddy place.

Grace followed up her monologue on Ford's delinquent childhood with, "He lied, stole, damaged property and generally caused trouble wherever he went. *That's* what everyone remembers when they hear the name Ford McCabe."

Dora continued working on the vibrant bouquet for Mrs. Lord. "I'll admit that's quite a track record, but people change, Grace."

"I know that," she admitted quietly. "But folks only remember the rebellious way he was and how much strife he'd caused. It might be unfair and judgmental, but I suppose those bad memories are all they have to go on." Even she could easily recall the reckless, recalcitrant kid he'd been, but she also remembered the vulnerability and loneliness in his eyes when she'd first met him. Beneath all that tough rebellion had been a boy aching to be loved, and accepted. She'd given him both, at the expense of her own reputation.

The irony of how history was about to repeat itself wasn't lost on Grace.

It was evident Ford *had* changed. His confidence and wealthy appearance showed a man who'd gained success. Yet, like everyone else, Grace felt so uncertain of him, his motives for returning, and why he'd chosen the very town that had spurned him to build such a sprawling, permanent kind of home.

And then there was her father, whose opinion of Ford hadn't changed or softened at all over the years. If anything, his bitterness and hatred had only grown for the man he believed was responsible for Aaron's death, his wife's demise, and tainting his young daughter's reputation. There was no forgiving, no compromising, and certainly no understanding how Grace had gotten herself into her current predicament.

Grace's chest banded with the awful possibility that she'd driven a permanent wedge between her and her father. Needing to release the pressure of holding in her father's disappointment of her actions, she said, "I finally told my father this morning about me and Ford."

Dora immediately glanced up from her task of arranging fern in the bouquet. "Nothing like waiting until the last minute," she said wryly. "How did it go?"

"Horribly." She couldn't stem the rush of tears that filled her eyes. She'd remained strong and adamant in front of her father while he'd ranted and raved and cursed Ford like a madman. Ellis's face had flushed with anger, and he'd clutched his heart as if she were breaking it. She'd remained immune to his theatrics and rage, refusing to allow her father to heap guilt upon her, but now, her fortitude dissolved. She'd needed her father's support, if not his understanding, and she'd gotten nothing but grief.

She swiped at a tear that escaped the corner of her eye. "He was furious about me marrying Ford, of course, and totally devastated about me being pregnant with Ford's child. He all but disowned me."

"Aw, Grace," Dora murmured, compassion glimmering in her eyes. "I'm sure your father will come around."

"I'm not too sure about that. In his eyes, I'm marrying the enemy, the man who destroyed his family and is now stealing his daughter, too." She sniffled, and drew a breath that seemed to shudder right to the depths of her soul. "I'm sure it's just a matter of a day or two before the entire town finds out I'm Ford's wife and that I married him because I'm pregnant with his baby. Considering how everyone feels about his return, I might as well wear a scarlet letter on my chest."

Dora laughed lightly at Grace's attempt at humor. "I'm sure there will be people who will be shocked, and your marriage will no doubt fuel the gossip, but a few weeks from now I'm sure the novelty of you being married to the town's bad boy will lose its appeal and everything will settle back down to normal."

Grace shot her friend a dubious look.

Dora wasn't the least bit daunted. "Grace, if Ford really has changed, then people have got to acknowledge that and accept him for the person he is now."

Grace remained silent and watched as Dora made a big fat bow out of red ribbon for Mrs. Lord's bouquet while one very important question persisted in her mind...who *was* Ford now?

The bell above the door tinkled, and Grace and Dora turned to see who'd entered the flower shop. Despite her dreary morning, Grace found an easy smile radiating within her at the sight of one of her most favorite people, Gertie Tedder, who owned the popular Gertie's Café in that strip of businesses near After Hours. She'd known Gertie all her life, and the plump older woman was the closest thing she'd ever had to a grandmother.

Gertie's green eyes lit up as they took in Grace's pink suit. "Well, don't you look as pretty as a picture today."

Grace's cheeks warmed, and she suddenly felt too

self-conscious in her wedding attire, as casual as it was. "Gertie, what are you doing here?" she asked, taking the attention off herself.

The older woman pushed through the low swinging gate to the work area and set a white bakery bag on the wooden bench. "Well, my joints were stiffening up some, so the bossy old man told me to take a walk, and since I had two cinnamon twists left over from this morning's batch, I thought I'd come see my two favorite girls."

"You're a sweet thing, Gertie," Dora said, enthusiastically opening the bakery bag and pulling out a fresh, fragrant twist for Grace, then one for herself.

Not sure if her stomach was in the mood for something so heavy, Grace set hers on a napkin.

"So, who's getting married?" Gertie asked abruptly.

Grace transferred a startled glance the older woman's way. "Uh, what makes you ask that?"

Gertie motioned to the items on the workbench. "Nosegays mean one of two things in Whitaker Falls—a school dance, or a wedding, and the prom just passed."

"Grace and Ford McCabe are getting married today," Dora announced around a mouthful of Gertie's confection.

Grace scowled at Dora, but there was nothing she could do about the news her assistant had imparted. After dealing with her father's censure this morning, she didn't think she could handle Gertie's disapproval, too.

"Ford McCabe, hmm?" Gertie asked, surprise and something more bemused in her tone. "Out of all the eligible men in Whitaker Falls, you had to stir up a ruckus with the town's rebel? And here I thought you were a good girl.''

The teasing note to Gertie's voice made Grace relax and smile. "I *am* a good girl. I just had a momentary lapse in judgment.'' Then she grew serious, wanting Gertie to hear everything from her, rather than through gossip. "I'm pregnant with his baby.''

Gertie just smiled, a knowing twinkle in her eyes. "I'm thinking you never stopped caring about Ford McCabe.''

The woman's insight caught Grace off guard. "Excuse me?''

"Oh, you never fooled me, sweetie-pie, when you'd ask me about Ford and his mama, and why everyone treated Ford so badly.'' She touched Grace's back in a soothing, comforting gesture and continued. "And I know those day old loaves of bread and cakes and cookies I gave you to take home never made it to your mother, either. One day, I saw you sneaking off toward Cutter Creek with my white bag in hand, and I knew…''

She silently thanked Gertie for her loyalty, and for never saying anything to her parents about her trysts to Cutter Creek. "His mother hardly ever bought groceries for Ford,'' she said, attempting to justify what she'd done. "And I felt sorry for him.''

"Yeah, I suppose it started out that way, out of the goodness of your heart.'' Picking up the crown of roses and baby's breath, Gertie placed the wreath on top of Grace's upswept hair, arranging it just so. "But then the look in your eyes changed when you mentioned Ford. You spoke of him with that soft, girlish catch in your breath and an unmistakable softness in your eyes.''

And despite everything, Grace still felt that girlish excitement when it came to Ford, and a very womanly desire that held too many emotions attached to it. "Gertie...do you harbor ill feelings toward Ford?"

Gertie appeared genuinely perplexed by her question. "Whatever for?"

"For all the terrible things he did when he was a kid?"

The older woman continued to arrange the wreath of flowers on Grace's head, then loosened wisps of hair from the top-knot she'd worn so a few tendrils curled around her face. "I didn't condone what he did, but I also understood that he was a very troubled boy. He didn't have an easy life, and the residents of Whitaker Falls didn't try to make his life any different or better, either." The frown of disapproval creasing Gertie's brow was no doubt for the narrow-minded people who'd treated Ford with nothing but contempt.

After a moment, Gertie's expression softened. "You make a beautiful bride, Grace."

Craving the emotional support she knew Gertie could offer her, Grace asked, "Would you do me a favor?"

"If it's within my power to grant, sweetie-pie."

Grace bit her lower lip nervously. "Could you... would you...be a witness at my wedding today?"

"I'd love to." Gertie's smile encompassed Grace in its warmth and affection. Her gaze sparkled with mischief. "That would give me a chance to make sure your young man's intentions are honorable."

Grace laughed, feeling more optimistic than she had in weeks. It was nice to know she had an ally in Gertie.

Would nothing in his life ever be easy or simple, Ford wondered as he stared into Grace's upturned face as Reverend Jones recited traditional wedding vows that would bind the woman standing before him as his wife. She looked beautiful in her pale pink outfit, the wreath of roses and baby's breath haloing her head and soft tendrils of hair framing her face. The bouquet of flowers in her hand trembled ever so slightly, giving testimony to the nerves and reluctance shimmering in her honey-brown gaze.

It seemed as though his marriage to Grace wouldn't be simple or easy, either.

Ford had envisioned a new beginning when he'd made the decision to move back to Whitaker Falls, a life full of promise and the opportunity to put the horrible memories of his past to rest. The goals he'd imagined had included Grace on some level, because she was a big part of why he'd returned, but he never would have guessed that fate would bring them together the way it had.

His gaze flickered briefly over the plump, grandmotherly woman standing next to Grace, dressed in a plain blue cotton dress, her hands folded in front of her ample waist, watching over Grace like a mother hen. When she'd first arrived, the other woman had shaken his hand in a firm grip and welcomed him back to Whitaker Falls—one of the few people who'd been warm to him since his return.

The past week had been interesting, and frustrating for Ford. He'd experienced varying degrees of shock and surprise that he was back and living out at Cutter Creek, along with animosity and outright hostility. People watched him as if they expected him to sprout horns, and others whispered his transgressions behind his back and speculated about *why* he'd returned. A few folks had no qualms about resurrecting old, bitter grudges and confronting him with them, after which he'd sincerely apologized for whatever sin he'd committed as a youth, and continued on his way. It was all he could do, until time proved that he'd become a decent, law-abiding citizen.

Though he couldn't fault any of them for being cautious and wary, their behavior only confirmed that nothing had really changed in Whitaker Falls... yet so much *would* change, starting here and now with Grace.

Following Reverend Jones's instructions, Ford picked up Grace's left hand and slipped a sparkling diamond bridal set on her slender ring finger, which he'd bought for her at an exclusive jewelry store in Richmond that past week. A shocked gasp caught in her throat as she stared at the elegant band of princess-cut diamonds that tiered to a one-carat flawless stone. Suppressing a smile, Ford tipped her chin back up, wanting to look into her eyes while they promised to love, honor and cherish each other—until death did they part. That was a pledge he intended to keep. She believed he was marrying her for the baby she carried, and though that was a good portion of the reason, he silently admitted that he'd dreamed too many times to count of making Grace completely his.

Reverend Jones finally closed his Bible, and glanced at the newly married couple. "By the power vested in me, I now pronounce you man and wife."

Ford's gaze dropped to Grace's sensual mouth as he waited impatiently for the good reverend to give him permission to kiss his new bride. As her husband, that was one privilege he planned to take advantage of. But much to Ford's disappointment, Reverend Jones only said, "Congratulations to the both of you."

Before Ford could take it upon himself to perform the traditional seal-of-vows kiss—and he'd been seconds away from taking matters into his own hands—Grace turned toward Gertie, putting a major crimp in Ford's plan.

Grace embraced the older woman in an affectionate hug. "Thank you for coming, Gertie," Grace said, her tone heartfelt and quivering with emotion. "It meant a lot to me to have you here."

"There's no way I could have refused you," Gertie replied, her green eyes suspiciously moist. Then she turned toward Ford and shook her finger at him. "You take real good care of my girl, you hear?"

The woman's fierce protectiveness amused and touched Ford. "I intend to, Gertie," he promised.

"See that you do, or else you'll answer to me." The stern lecture ebbed into a fond, amicable smile. "Now, I insist that the two of you come by the café so I can feed you both before you go home. No sense having to worry about cooking on your wedding night."

The relief Ford detected in Grace's expression was unmistakable, making him realize that she'd been worried about more than cooking a meal on her wedding night—she was nervous about being alone with him.

There was no reason for her to be skittish around him, because he planned to make their arrangement as easy on her as possible—no barbaric marital demands, and no unrealistic expectations. He'd only take what he could coax her to willingly give him.

He wanted her trust, and he intended to secure it; he'd need every ounce of her support and faith for what lay ahead.

"You settling in okay?"

Ford's deep, rumbling voice caused a shiver to ripple down Grace's spine, prompting her to glance over her shoulder. She found him lounging in the doorway of the guest bedroom, still wearing the chocolate-colored slacks he'd donned for the ceremony, but the matching jacket was gone, and so was his tie. The first three buttons of his white dress shirt were undone, and he'd cuffed his sleeves to reveal strong, tanned forearms.

Despite her resolve to maintain her emotional distance from him, her heart fluttered beneath her breast. The man was too sexy and appealing for her peace of mind.

"I'm settling in just fine," she said, valiantly trying to concentrate on the task of putting away the clothing, toiletries and other personal items that they'd picked up from her cottage on the way out to his house at Cutter Creek.

"Good." He smiled amicably, producing one of those gorgeous dimples that made her pulse race. "I want you to be comfortable, since this is your house now, too."

With a sweep of her hand she indicated the queen-size bed covered in a plain hunter-green spread and mahogany dresser against the far wall. "This is great." The room was a bit on the masculine side, and simply decorated, but she was certain once she brought over some of her things it would feel and look more like the feminine haven she'd grown used to at the cottage.

She was still surprised, and relieved, that Ford hadn't argued when she'd requested the guest room next to his huge master bedroom, though the rogue had pointed out that the arrangement seemed a bit incongruous, considering that they'd already shared a bed. Ultimately, he'd respected her wishes with minimal fuss, and that's all she cared about. She wasn't trying to make their relationship difficult, just bearable for her. She wasn't ready to share nightly intimacies with a man she was uncertain of. If she had to spend the rest of her life with Ford, then she planned to learn *everything* about him, past, present and future, before giving him free access to her heart, body and soul.

He slipped his hands into the pockets of his trousers, his stance casual and relaxed as he watched her. "You know, I have to confess, I thought the wedding ceremony was lacking."

She shrugged while tucking a stack of T-shirts into the dresser drawer. "The ceremony was short, simple and to the point."

"But...lacking," he insisted.

The light from the lamp on the dresser caught the ring on her finger, dazzling her with a thousand-watt sparkle. There was certainly nothing lacking about the extravagant, and obviously expensive bridal set he'd chosen for her to wear. "We promised to honor and cherish each other, until death do we part. What more could you possibly want?"

"What more could I possibly want..." he repeated the question thoughtfully, as if pondering a multitude of wicked desires. Pushing off the doorjamb, he strolled slowly toward her. His stride was lazy, but the gleam in his smoky violet eyes was very masculine and filled with purpose. "How about to kiss my bride?"

Awareness zinged to life within her, and she moved to the bed where her suitcase lay open, putting distance between them before he trapped her near the dresser. "That's not a necessary part of the ceremony." Damning her quivering voice when she wanted to appear unaffected by him, she picked up the silk chemise she slept in and folded it, keeping her hands busy.

"It's necessary to me," he said, coming up behind her.

He didn't touch her, but she could feel the heat of his body down the length of her back. The warmth of his breath tickled the fine hairs at her nape, and the citrusy cologne he wore made her senses spin. Her nerves tripped all over themselves, and a rush of pure, undiluted longing nearly overwhelmed her.

His hand appeared at the side of her waist, and he gently tugged her nightgown from her idle fingers, repositing the slip of silk into her half-empty suitcase. His large palm flattened on her abdomen, slid gently around her waist, pressing her back to his chest.

She swallowed, hard, but didn't move.

"Kissing the bride is a tradition," he said, his low voice rumbling near her ear. "And it's a nice way to seal the vows we took." With a subtle pressure, he coaxed her to turn around in his embrace, keeping their bodies flush by splaying a hand low on her spine. "I'd really like to kiss my bride," he murmured, his gaze fixed on her mouth.

Her hands curled around his arms, mainly because

she didn't know what to do with them. Through the sensual fog quickly settling over her, she realized that Ford was asking for her permission, not taking what he believed was his due. That knowledge chipped away at her will to resist him. But she knew what happened when they kissed, knew that every responsible thought short-circuited once their lips touched, and she did very foolish things. She clung to that shred of instinct, tried desperately to ignore the warm, large hand stroking over her bottom, urging her intimately closer.

"I really don't think we should." The husky quality of her voice made a mockery of her words.

He lowered his head, placing a soft, chaste kiss on the corner of her mouth, making her ache for more. His lips skimmed to her neck, the tip of his tongue tasting and teasing…

Her control slipped a serious notch. Closing her eyes, she automatically angled her head, giving his mouth more access to her throat. A delicate shiver coursed through her when he discovered a particularly sensitive spot and nibbled gently. Seemingly of their own accord, her hands fluttered upward, sliding into the hair at the back of his neck to keep him from pulling away.

"One kiss, Grace," he whispered, undisguised need roughening his voice. "As man and wife."

Her lips parted, but there was no protest forthcoming this time, just breathless anticipation for the pleasure of his tempting, insatiable kisses. His mouth returned to hers, putting a match to the sensual wildfire simmering between them.

The kiss he gave her was slow and deep, exciting and ravenous, and very thorough. He tasted like the chocolate cream pie Gertie had served them after their meal, rich and sensuous and deliciously decadent.

Searing heat settled in the pit of her belly. As her husband, he took liberties she found too pleasurable to deny him, or herself. While his soft, warm lips kept hers occupied in a series of provocative, heady kisses, he skimmed a hand up her rib cage and filled his palm with her breast through her silk blouse and lacy bra, squeezing gently, then flicked his thumb over the sensitive tip. A tiny moan rumbled in her throat, startling her with the undertones of hunger and need it evoked. She wanted Ford, but she didn't want to want him!

He must have sensed her shift in mood, because he brought their kiss to an end. By the time he lifted his head, a satisfied smile curved his mouth. "*Now* I feel married," he said, a teasing light in his eyes.

And she felt dazed, and on the brink of surrendering to dangerous emotions. She glanced away, ashamed at her lack of control when it came to Ford.

His fingers touched her jaw in concern. "Hey, are you okay?"

She summoned a smile to match how weary she felt. "I'm just tired."

His hands settled on the waistband of her skirt, his thumbs brushing along her slightly curved, firm belly, sending tingles skittering along the surface of her skin. "The baby?" he asked.

Slipping from his unnerving embrace, and away from his tempting touch, she rubbed her forehead. "It's been a very long day, Ford."

"Grace..." He let out a low, frustrated sigh. "I know we started off on the wrong foot, and I know you're not happy with this situation, but I'm willing to make the best of our marriage. Will you agree to just try to compromise? For the sake of our child?''

She wanted to ask him if that kiss had been for the sake of their child, but bit back the petty remark. Her emotions and hormones were askew, her heart unsure of what she'd gotten herself into by marrying Ford—a man she'd known all her life, but a stranger she wasn't quite sure she trusted nonetheless.

''I'd do *anything* for this baby,'' she said, meaning every word, and giving him a silent promise to try to meet him halfway on marital issues. She grabbed her chemise, robe and toiletry bag. ''I think I'll take a nice warm shower, and turn in for the evening.''

He gave her a smile that was boyishly charming. ''Would you like help scrubbing your back?''

That treacherous heat unfurled in her belly. ''No, thank you.''

''Can't blame a husband for asking, especially on his wedding night,'' he said, backing toward the door. ''If you need me for anything, I'll be in my office down the hall working.''

Then he was gone, leaving Grace to spend her wedding night alone, and lonely.

CHAPTER SIX

"GOOD morning."

Grace turned from the task of making herself a second mug of hot tea to go with the toast she'd just eaten, the greeting she'd been about to return dissolving on the tip of her tongue.

Her husband strode very deliberately across the kitchen's hardwood floor toward her, giving her only a handful of seconds to register the fact that he'd just gotten out of the shower. His dark hair was damp and finger-combed away from his face, and he only wore a pair of soft, faded jeans that enhanced his athletic body. His feet were bare, his chest gloriously naked with drops of water still clinging to the light furring of hair that sprinkled its way down to his belly, whorled around his navel, and disappeared into the waistband of his low, hip-riding jeans.

The man had no right to look so sexy, so appealing, so downright tempting and gorgeously male! Especially first thing in the morning.

She dragged her gaze upward, too late to realize he'd closed the distance between them. Without preamble or warning, he slid his fingers into her unbound, disheveled hair, lifted her mouth to his and kissed her. Unlike last night's slow seduction, there was nothing sweet or chaste about this possession. His strong, masculine body crowded her against the counter, his tongue took advantage of her gasp of surprise, and his fresh, mint-tasting mouth did deliciously wonderful things to hers.

She groaned deep in her throat and surrendered. It was all she *could* do.

Too soon, he let her go, stepping away from her as if they hadn't just shared a very passionate kiss that left her dizzy and breathless...and wanting more.

"Uh, good morning," she finally managed to say, her voice husky.

The corner of his mouth quirked, and his gaze slid down the length of her, a slow, lazy perusal that missed nothing and visually stripped away her robe and chemise beneath. How did he do that—make her feel as though his hands had stroked where his gaze had just lingered?

"It would have been an even better morning if I could have woken up with you in my bed," he said.

Sensual images of tangled sheets and entwined limbs filled her head, just as the rogue intended, no doubt. It dawned on her that her husband wasn't going to play fair about their sleeping arrangements.

Crossing her arms over her chest, she regarded him primly. "Do you plan to execute sneak attacks like that all the time?"

"Absolutely." He reached for a coffee mug in the cupboard, while looking over his shoulder at her. "Or are you going to place restrictions on how many times I can kiss you, and when or where?"

Where...as in location, or *where*...as in what body part? A shiver touched her feminine nerves, and she mentally shook the stimulating thought from her mind.

Setting the mug on the counter next to the coffeepot, he cast her a patient look. "I'm not demanding my conjugal rights, Grace, but you don't expect us to live under the same roof, and me be able to resist that mouth of yours, do you?"

The mouth in question still tingled from his kiss. The thought of giving Ford carte blanche to indulge his whimsical need to kiss her sent her pulse tumbling into oblivion...along with her refusal. She couldn't even believe they were having this conversation, or that she was considering his request! "I really don't think it would be a good idea—"

"I *can't* resist you, Grace," he interrupted, pouring steaming coffee into his cup. "I want the right to kiss you, whenever I want to."

She shook her head regretfully. "Ford—"

"What happened to compromise, Grace?" he chided, making her feel a twinge of guilt for being so difficult over something that shouldn't have been a big issue or problem in their marriage. "Considering making love to you seems to be off limits for the time being, you can't expect me to go *completely* without physical contact. I have needs and urges like any other married man when it comes to my wife. I'm not asking you to share my bed, though I'd welcome you there any time and the invitation is always open. I only want the privilege to kiss my wife."

He made his argument sound so simple, so innocent, and she was being so difficult. It wasn't as though his kisses were a hardship to endure, and they did give her as much pleasure as they brought him. Certainly the affection and tenderness that came with kissing could only enhance their relationship without the demand of more physical intimacies.

"All right," she agreed. "Kisses only."

He moved back toward her, and her heart thumped in her chest, though she didn't try to avoid him—there was no sense in trying. He touched a finger to her bottom lip, the violet hue of his eyes darkening to velvet. "Any *time* I want 'em?" he asked, his voice low and rumbling.

Her stomach dipped and she forced herself to nod.

"Any *way* I want 'em?" His head tilted, moved closer to hers.

She nodded again, at the same time lifting her mouth toward the heat and promise of his. The anticipation of feeling his lips on hers became excruciating, and exciting.

His lashes fell half-mast. "Fair enough," he murmured in satisfaction, his breath caressing her lips.

Closing her eyes, she waited…and felt a sting of disappointment when he pressed a saintly kiss to her forehead. Her lashes blinked open, and she frowned, but he didn't notice. He was taking a sip of his coffee, looking for all the world as if he hadn't turned her inside out with wanting, then left her unsatisfied.

He propped a hip on the counter next to her. "How are you feeling this morning?"

She added more hot water to her mug of tea since it had cooled during her discussion with Ford, concentrating on the task. "Refreshed." And aroused, darn him! Having given him the right to kiss her, anytime, any way, and anywhere, she'd forever be in a state of awareness, anxiously awaiting when he'd plan his next sensual assault on her senses.

"Do you experience morning sickness?"

The genuine concern and curiosity in his voice surprised her. "Sometimes." Affecting the same casual attitude as he, she warmed to their subject, and his interest. "I find tea and toast usually curbs the nausea."

He nodded, and took a drink of coffee, lingering over the taste as his gaze seemingly searched the territory her robe and chemise covered. "Has your body changed much?"

Her face flushed at his bold question, but she was pleased that he wanted to share as much of this experience with her as possible. "My...breasts have gotten larger, and much firmer. And they're extremely sensitive."

"I noticed that last night."

She sipped her tea, needing the warmth to calm the flutters in her belly. "And my zip-up pants and skirts are beginning to feel a little snug. At this rate, I'll be showing in another month."

"I can't wait to see that," he said softly. Unmistakable yearning deepened his voice, and he quickly cleared his throat at that display of emotion. "You glow with happiness when you talk about the baby, you know."

She rested a hand protectively over her belly, admitting that she did feel an awesome, happy glow that seemed to radiate from the inside, out—and she hadn't even heard the baby's heartbeat or felt it move yet. "I never thought I'd be given the opportunity to have a child of my own."

"Of our own," he corrected mildly. "And I'm glad I could give you a baby. In fact, I'll give you as many as you want. After this baby is born, we can bend the rules a bit on our sleeping arrangement and work on number two."

His teasing tone prodded a tentative smile from

her, but she had no idea what the future held for them, and refused to commit to anything beyond the present. "How about we just take it one at a time?"

"You sure about that, Mrs. McCabe?" he said mischievously. "We could have months to practice…"

"I'm sure." Needing a quick change of subject, she asked, "Would you like some breakfast?"

"I'm a self-sufficient husband." Finishing off his coffee, he set the empty mug in the sink. "I don't need a huge breakfast in the mornings. A cup of coffee and a bowl of Frosted Flakes is all I need. You go sit down and relax."

Grace took a seat at the small oak table situated in a connecting breakfast nook. The floor-to-ceiling windows overlooked a newly built barn, corral and an expanse of green pasture. "Don't expect me to allow you to pass on those atrocious eating habits to our son or daughter."

"Then I guess that gives you the next six or seven months to reform me." He joined her at the table with his box of cereal, a large bowl and a carton of milk. "I'm very reformable, ya' know."

She sipped her tea, wondering about the different ways he'd reformed over the years and how he'd struggled to make a new, successful life for himself. So why would he return to the town that never once supported him? The question niggled her, but it wasn't something she wanted to dwell on right now.

Instead she focused on another subject she wanted to clarify. "Ford…did you mean what you said yesterday about keeping the cottage?" She'd thought he'd want to sell her house, considering his own place had room enough for ten, but he'd surprised her with a comment about using the cottage for a retreat.

"Of course I did." He filled his bowl with the sugar-coated flakes, and drowned them in milk. "It's obvious you love the place, and I think it would make a nice getaway for you, or both of us if you'd ever like. And our son or daughter would certainly love playing in that lake."

"Thank you," she said, meaning it. Though she'd only lived in the cottage for a few years, she'd grown to love the cozy place.

"I don't intend to take anything away from you, Grace. We'll move whatever furniture and knick-knacks you want into our house." He glanced around the kitchen while chewing a bite of cereal. Swallowing, he said, "I certainly wouldn't mind a woman's touch in the place. In fact, I'd appreciate it if you'd handle the decorating. I've got the bare essentials right now, but there's a whole lot of room for improvement."

He'd taken her on a brief tour when they'd first arrived yesterday afternoon, and though the furnishings were sparse, the structure was soundly built and it was evident no expense had been spared on the craftsmanship, fixtures, or cosmetic appearance. "It's a lovely house."

His gaze met hers. "It's more than I ever thought I'd have."

Finished with his breakfast, Ford stood and took his empty bowl to the sink and rinsed it out. He glanced out the window in front of him, then he looked back at Grace. "You didn't get to see much of the outside of the house yesterday. Would you like to take a morning stroll after breakfast and see the rest of the place?''

She realized that for all of Ford's confidence, he wanted *her* approval. She found she couldn't refuse him, or disappoint him. ''I'd like that,'' she said, hoping the comfortable relationship they were establishing would enable her to get to know him better. ''Give me half an hour to shower and change, and then I'm all yours for the day.''

Ford walked casually alongside Grace as they passed the empty corral he hoped someday soon to fill with a few quarter horses. A huge sense of contentment warmed him as he told her of his plans and they talked companionably about nothing in particular. They'd spent the past hour strolling around his property while he showed her the improvements he'd made to the land, and indicated his intentions for the future. She'd been suitably impressed, and he'd been filled with pride for all that he'd accomplished.

It was a heady sensation to realize just how far he'd come in eleven years. To an outsider looking in, he seemed to have it all: a sprawling home that exceeded anything in Whitaker Falls, a business that was flourishing, a beautiful wife and a baby on the way that would satisfy the craving he'd always had for a family of his own. Life couldn't get much sweeter for a man who'd spent his youth as a juvenile delinquent, struggling for acceptance, and resenting the fact that nobody cared enough about him to *try* to give him the guidance he'd so desperately needed.

But for all that he'd obtained, the one most important thing seemed to allude him—Grace. For all that she'd accepted their situation, she was still cautious with him. Not that he could blame her. Everything had happened so quickly between them, from his surprise return, to a whirlwind courtship that hadn't allowed time for them to discover who they'd become in the past eleven years. No amount of money would banish that reserve of hers, or gain her trust and respect...just time, care and a whole lot of patience...and those stolen kisses he'd insisted upon this morning.

He glanced at the woman beside him, and frowned. Though they'd only been outside for a short amount of time, she looked tired, her face flushed from the warm sunshine. Taking into consideration her delicate condition, he lightly grasped her elbow and steered her toward the house, and the sturdy, hand-carved oak swing he'd had installed on the back porch.

She settled herself on the swing, her brown eyes holding a combination of bewilderment and feminine curiosity.

He sat beside her, leaving a foot of space between them. "What's on your mind, Grace?" he asked, determined to find out what had his wife so perplexed.

She tilted her head, regarding him speculatively. "Out of all the places you could afford to live, why would you choose to return to Whitaker Falls?"

Her curiosity was certainly valid, since nothing had been easy or welcoming about his return. He'd concluded years ago that it would be much less complicated for him to build a house near Richmond, where people knew and acknowledged him for the successful businessman he was, yet he'd always known that he'd return to Whitaker Falls, despite the possible tribulation of doing so.

Stretching his arm across the back of the swing, he wove the tail end of her French braid between his fingers, unable to resist touching her. "I know it seems crazy, coming back to the one place where I'm least wanted, and everyone associates the name 'McCabe' with disgrace, scandal and a list of offenses, but my reasons for returning are pretty basic and unpretentious, actually." He paused for a moment, hoping she'd understand his motivations, as foolish as they suddenly seemed to be. "Cutter Creek is where my roots are."

That seemed to surprise her. "You came back because you grew up here?"

"Yeah." It was as simple, and as complex as that. He tried to explain. "This land belonged to my grandparents, then my mother, and even though she didn't care enough to try to hang on to the only legacy she had, it was *my* legacy, too. Cutter Creek is a part of who I am." Bitterness seeped into his tone, and he swallowed it back, refusing to allow those resentful emotions to intrude on what had started out as a pleasant day. "I couldn't see someone else living here, when I've always wanted this land for my own, to build a big house and raise a family here."

The understanding he sought touched her expression and softened her gaze, giving him the fortitude to continue.

"I wanted to come back and make a difference in the McCabe lineage," he said, giving her a glimpse of the vulnerability he'd hadn't been able to shake over the years. "Everybody remembers my drunk of a mother who practically lived at the After Hours bar, and this scrappy, illegitimate kid who caused trouble wherever he went. I want this time around to be different."

She pushed the swing into a slow, swaying motion with the toe of her sandal. "You can't change the past, Ford."

"No, I can't change the past," he agreed, trailing his fingers over her shoulder in a light caress. "But I've learned that I'm in control of my future, and that's where I'm going to make the difference, here at Cutter Creek. I've spent the past eleven years working hard, trying to prove to myself that I could be something, despite how I grew up. Getting to where I am today hasn't been easy, but every struggle has been worth it." He wasn't defensive, just adamant about using his success to his advantage.

"And now you have your own business, which I'm assuming is doing well for itself," she said, clasping her hands over her stomach. At his silent nod, she prompted, "So what, exactly, does FZM do?"

Remembering how vague he'd been about his business during his dinner date with Grace, and how cautious he still needed to be, he chose his words wisely. "It's a development company. The company I originally went to work for when I left here, Khann and Associates, gave me the financial backing and support I needed to start the company a few years ago. Khann is like a silent investor. I bid on the projects and develop them, and the profits are split. I'm in the process of acquiring a piece of property I plan to redevelop, which will be my first project without Khann's financial backing.'' And until he was awarded the piece of land, that's all he was willing to reveal.

"Will your work keep you away from home much?" she asked.

Home. He liked the way that sounded. "I hope not. I've got a main office in Richmond, with a secretary who keeps all my paperwork and bookkeeping in order, and two project managers who oversee my jobs. I'm sure I'll be spending at least three days a week in Richmond to keep an eye on things, but I can work on a bid or proposal here at the house just as easily as I can at the main office. I've got a computer, fax, copier, phone and every other modern office convenience to run things smoothly from here."

"Well, I'll try to stay out of your way as much as possible," she said, wrapping a hand around the chain-link holding up her end of the swing. "Grace and Charm keeps me pretty busy, so you'll have the house to yourself during the day."

"You won't ever be in my way," he assured her, leaning closer and bypassing that one-foot safety zone he'd kept between them. "Besides, I wouldn't mind having you nearby, just in case I get an uncontrollable urge to kiss you."

Her lips parted and her eyes widened slightly in anticipation. Deciding to let the desire and craving for his kiss simmer for the time being, he merely ran a finger down the slope of her nose.

She let out a puff of air, flustered and exasperated by his playful tactics. "You, Ford McCabe, are a terrible tease."

He laughed warmly, feeling confident everything

would work out okay between them—even if they
did have to deal with the town's scrutiny and opinion of their marriage.

Grace blew out a disgusted stream of breath, and
closed the bookkeeping journal for Grace and
Charm Flower Shop. Four weeks of being married
to Ford, and her business was down by over forty
percent. She thanked goodness for her standing orders for weekly arrangements for the country club
and the bank, which were keeping her afloat. But
she depended on unexpected walk-in and phone orders to supplement her income.

When she'd first noticed the decrease in orders a
few weeks ago, Dora assured her it was the warm
weather keeping customers away, but Grace knew
better than to believe that placating excuse. The tension that had developed in town since she'd married
Ford, and the news of her impending pregnancy, was
palpable. Oh, people she'd grown up with were polite enough to her when she addressed them, but
they didn't go out of their way to be sociable or
congenial. There were a few individuals she'd encountered who'd outright expressed their disapproval and hostility to her alliance with Ford and
reminded her of Ford's nefarious crimes as a youth.

The majority of the community was certain Ford
had returned to cause more trouble, despite his respectable presence, and what he'd achieved over the
years. Few believed a hoodlum like him could ever
change, and she hated that she had to lump her own
father into that category.

Closing her eyes, she rested her elbows on the
surface of her desk and rubbed at the slow throb

beginning in her temples. She'd seen her father four times since marrying Ford, and each visit had ended the same way, with Ellis cursing the man who was now her husband and issuing an ultimatum Grace refused to accept.

Ironically, she understood her father's bitterness toward Ford, who, in Ellis's mind, had destroyed his family, and who now had taken his daughter away from him, too. More than anything, she loved her father, but she would not choose between him and the man she'd married, no matter how torn and hurt the situation made her. She had a child's welfare to consider, and refused to penalize Ford for wanting to give this baby a better life than what he'd endured. All she could do was hope in time that her father's resentment toward Ford ebbed, because it would be his grandchild who would suffer in the future.

Feeling claustrophobic in her small office, and needing fresh air to clear her aching head, Grace made the spontaneous decision to go to the one place that seemed to bring her calm and peace, which she desperately needed right now.

Clearing her desk and picking up her purse, Grace headed into the work area. Dora sat on the padded stool in front of the cash register counter, immersed in a romance novel. All orders for the day had been filled, and the place was spotless, so Grace had encouraged her assistant to take advantage of the lull in business.

"Could you close up the shop for me this evening, Dora?" Grace asked.

Dora glanced up from the book she was reading,

her dreamy expression flowing into a concerned frown. "Sure, Grace. Everything okay?"

"Everything is as good as it's going to get for now," she said wryly. Slinging the long strap of her purse over her shoulder, she slid open the refrigeration unit housing their flowers and premade arrangements and stepped inside, surveying what she had available, which was a whole lot more than normal. "I think I need to spend some time with my mother and brother," she said, glancing over her shoulder at her assistant.

A smile canted Dora's mouth. She'd come to understand Grace's visits to her mother's and brother's grave sites as therapeutic. "Tell them hello for me."

"Oh, they're getting an earful today, but I'll try to fit your greeting in." Returning Dora's smile, Grace stepped out of the unit with a gorgeous arrangement of roses and baby's breath for her mother, and a bouquet of bright daisies and yellow and orange carnations for her brother.

Just as she exited the flower shop, Ford pulled his car into the empty slot in front of her business. Curious as to why he was there when he'd told her that morning he'd be returning from Richmond later that evening, Grace stopped and waited as he slid out of the vehicle and came toward her. He was dressed impeccably in toffee-colored slacks, a silky dress shirt in brown tones and Italian loafers. The intent in his violet eyes caused her heart to race.

Her hands were full, and she had a sudden sneaking suspicion that he planned to take advantage of that fact. Sure enough, he reached her and immediately slipped his arms around her waist, engulfing her in an intimate, chest-to-thigh embrace. The kind of clinch lovers shared. Her breath hitched in her throat, the arrangements trembled in her hands, and her bones liquified as she read the *anytime, anywhere* dare in his eyes.

He unceremoniously kissed her, heedless of the people walking by on the sidewalk, or anyone watching from neighboring businesses. Since their marriage had already caused a scandal and widespread gossip, and Grace enjoyed Ford's romantic kisses, she didn't issue an ounce of objection of her husband's silent challenge. His warm lips slipped over hers, parting them, seeking a deeper contact. She moaned, not in protest, but delicious surrender, and returned the sizzling kiss.

It was over as fast as it had begun, but left a lasting impression on the people watching them, most of whom appeared shocked at Ford's brazen display of affection. Grace figured that was Ford's strategy, to lay claim to her publicly, and she'd done nothing to stop him.

"Here, let me take those for you," he said easily, as if he hadn't just scattered her senses with his kiss. He lifted the arrangements before they slipped from her fingers.

She stared up at him, trying to gather her bearings. "What are you doing here? I thought you had an afternoon meeting in Richmond and you weren't going to be home until later tonight."

He shrugged. "My meeting didn't last as long as I thought it would."

There was something in his eyes she couldn't pinpoint. "Everything okay?"

"Yep." He flashed her a reassuring smile. "Just trying to tie up some details of the property I'm trying to acquire," he said dismissively, then indicated the bouquets he held. "Where are you off to? A delivery?"

Didn't she wish. Not wanting to reveal her depressing business problems, she kept her tone light. "I thought I'd take some flowers out to Aaron and my mother."

His expression grew somber when he realized what she meant. "Would you mind if I go with you?" His voice was low, and slightly rough with emotion.

She'd thought she needed this time alone, but the susceptible emotions she detected in Ford's eyes tugged at her heart. She clearly recalled the day of Aaron's funeral, and how Ford had stood yards away from the crowd of mourners at her brother's grave site, knowing he wasn't welcome to be a part of the group when he'd been blamed for Aaron's death. Through her tears of sorrow, she'd looked out across the distance separating them, seeing a boy who'd spent his life trying to fit in, but always ended up alone.

She'd wanted to go to him, comfort him in his grief, but hadn't dared. Instead she'd watched him swipe at his eyes as they'd lowered her brother's casket into the ground, then he'd turned and walked away...and left Whitaker Falls.

She couldn't say no, couldn't deny Ford the chance to make peace with a part of his past. "Yeah, I think Aaron would like that."

CHAPTER SEVEN

"Do you come out here often?"

Grace brushed away the dirt that had settled on her mother's headstone and placed her bouquet of roses at the base. "A few times a month," she said, casting a glance at Ford, who stood behind her, hands buried in the pockets of his slacks, watching as she tended to her mother's and brother's grave sites. He seemed uncomfortable now that they were at the cemetery, as if he wasn't sure what to do or how to act.

Having spent the past eleven years visiting her mother and brother, she tried to put Ford at ease. "I know this might sound strange, but I find it comforting to just sit under this shady tree and talk to them about things that might be bothering me, or things I think they'd like to know. It makes me feel close to them."

An awkward moment passed before he tentatively asked, "Do they know about us?"

"Yeah, they know everything," she admitted with some amusement as she plucked away a few stray weeds from Aaron's marker before they had a chance to spread. Sitting back on her heels, she drew a deep breath, trying to stem a sudden tide of sorrow that hadn't lessened over the years. "It seems like it was only yesterday that they died, and I still miss them terribly."

"I'm sorry," he said, his compassion evident in his gentle tone.

Standing, she smoothed a hand down the skirt of her light cotton dress, accepting the condolence he offered. She suspected he still carried around his share of grief for the loss of his friend. Strolling over to the trunk of the huge tree that shaded her mother's and brother's graves, she picked up the checkered blanket she'd taken from her vehicle before they'd gotten into Ford's car for the drive out to Ridgecrest Cemetery. Snapping open the blanket, she sat down in one corner, hoping Ford would join her.

He didn't. He kept staring at Aaron's headstone.

"I often wonder what Aaron would be doing now if he'd lived," she said, trying to fill the silence that had settled over them. "My father wanted him to go on to college and follow in his footsteps as a physician, but I just can't see that."

Ford's head turned to look at her, his expression grim. "I'm sure your father believes it was my bad influence that kept Aaron from going on to college."

"Possibly, as an excuse for the truth."

A dark brow lifted, but the muscles across his shoulders remained tense. "Which was?"

"Aaron wasn't interested in being a doctor, but my father didn't want to believe that." She curled her legs to the side and tucked her dress around them. "At nineteen, I don't think *Aaron* knew what he wanted to do with his life."

The pain and hostility of the past lurked in Ford's gaze. "I'm sure Aaron befriending me didn't help matters."

"Aaron liked you. He thought you were wild and

rebellious, just like the rest of us did, but Aaron always saw the good in others.''

''As you do.''

The soft way he said the words made her heart catch. So few people had taken the time and care to see past Ford's defiance to the insecure boy he'd been. In that moment, she realized her and Aaron's friendship had made a difference in Ford's solitary world, had possibly given him the first bit of confidence to straighten out his life.

''Finding good in others is a trait we inherited from our mother,'' she said, giving credit where it was due. ''She always believed in giving people chances, while my father has always been one to cling to first impressions. I'm glad I got my mother's more generous nature.''

''Yeah, me, too. And thank goodness for second chances, or else you would have run screaming that day you came out to Cutter Creek looking for Aaron.''

Ford's idle comment faded the present into the past, bringing to Grace's mind the first day she'd met Ford face-to-face. She'd been out to save her brother's hide after witnessing her father ranting and raving about Aaron hanging out with Ford, and how Ellis was going to ''whip him'' when he returned home. Grace had snuck out of the house on the pretense of going to Gertie's, and instead made her first trip out to the McCabe homestead in search of her brother. Ford had answered the door of the tiny dilapidated house, and immediately turned belligerent and defensive about her being there. When Grace had explained she was looking for Aaron, Ford admitted that he wasn't there, and he honestly didn't know where he was.

That day forged the fragile beginning of a friendship between them, and soon she found herself sneaking out to Cutter Creek to be with Ford, at first just to offer him companionship. But somewhere along the way their platonic feelings for one another had developed into so much more. Casual touches led to sensual feelings, which led to those deep, intimate kisses Ford spent hours teaching her, which eventually evolved into emotions and needs neither one of them had been able to suppress.

In a few months, she'd watched Ford struggle to shed the antagonistic reputation he'd earned and try to redeem himself, *for her,* he'd told her. But no one else believed him capable of changing, no one gave him the chance to prove he could. Getting a job had been impossible; everyone knew Ford McCabe lied, cheated and stole.

And then he'd killed Aaron, or so everyone believed.

She glanced up at Ford, who still stood too far away. The breeze tousled his dark hair, and he pushed his fingers through the thick mass as his gaze lingered on Aaron's plot.

Drawing her knees up to her chest, Grace wrapped her arms around them. "Remember that day at my cottage when you asked me if I blamed you for Aaron's death?"

He didn't look her way. "Yeah."

"I don't," she said, wanting, needing him to know that she always believed he'd been wrongly accused. "I never have."

He glanced at her finally, bitter memories haunting his beautiful violet eyes. "What if I am to blame, like everyone believes?"

"What happened was an accident, Ford, at least according to the police report." She frowned as his meaning became clear. "Are you suggesting that you *were* responsible for his death?"

His self-recrimination was evident in the hardening of his jaw. "Only because I was behind the wheel that night."

Other than the brief details he'd divulged to the police, no one really knew what had transpired the night Aaron had died, except for Ford. "Will you tell me what happened?"

Grief and regret twisted his features, making Grace ache for him.

"Come sit down and tell me," she said, smoothing her hand over the blanket next to her. "Please?"

Ford hesitated, torn between withholding the awful memories of that long-ago night, and releasing the burden he'd carried for eleven long years. Feeling weary to the bone, he made his way to the woman who'd become his wife, and settled himself next to her. Then he mentally thrust himself back to that cold winter night that had changed his life forever.

"Your brother was drunk the night of the accident, but I was completely sober," he said, wanting that speculation cleared right up-front. The sheriff had tested him for alcohol immediately following the accident, and though he'd been cleared of that charge, no one had believed it. Everyone assumed he'd been the one out drinking and carousing, corrupting Aaron. "I'd gone to a party out in Pinewood with Richard Kip, and your brother was there, already having consumed more beers than he could remember having. He was in no shape to drive, so I took his car keys and insisted on driving him home.''

Raising his knees, he draped his wrists over them, dredging up the fortitude needed to relive the events that followed. ''On the way home, right out of Pinewood, I hit a patch of black ice and lost control of the car. The car flipped and rolled into a ravine, and because Aaron wasn't wearing a seat belt, the impact threw him from the vehicle.''

A shudder racked Ford's body as details filled his mind with vivid clarity. ''I must have been knocked unconscious when the car flipped into the ravine, because everything was so eerily quiet when I came to. When I realized what had happened, I managed to free myself and scrambled up the hill for Aaron. I found him sprawled on the road, and there was blood everywhere...'' His voice was ragged with emotion, his chest painfully tight. ''I made it to Aaron, but there was nothing I could do to save him. He took his last breath while I was holding him, begging him not to die. I've never felt more helpless in my entire life.''

Grace's hand touched his taut back in a soothing gesture. He glanced at her, and his heart caught at the tears and compassion brimming in her eyes. ''Oh, Ford, I never knew...''

No one had known, because he'd never revealed those personal, anguished details of the accident. Everyone had come to their own conclusions, and the horrible stories they'd concocted had all been pure speculation, fueling the town's censure toward him.

"I went to your brother's funeral to pay my respects," he went on, wanting her to know everything. "I was completely devastated by his death and only wanted to offer my condolences. But as soon as people saw me approaching the grave site, the animosity toward me was tangible, so I kept my distance. Then I saw the pure venom and hatred in your father's eyes, and I knew it was time to leave Whitaker Falls. I never meant to hurt you, Grace, I just knew I couldn't stay and face more condemnation."

She nodded emphatically. "That first year you were gone was a difficult one for us," she admitted softly. "My father suffered a heart attack from all the stress of losing Aaron, and my mother was so devastated by Aaron's death that when she contracted pneumonia, she didn't even try to fight to live. She died within a year of Aaron, which nearly destroyed my father."

"And what about you?"

"Emotionally, I was a mess, but someone had to be strong." She offered him a smile that didn't quite reach her shadowed gaze, making him wonder what she wasn't revealing. She didn't give him the chance to ask, and instead said, "Thanks for sharing everything with me."

"Thanks for listening." As a result, his soul did feel lighter, freer. "Can I come out here with you again sometime?"

Her expression softened with sweet acceptance. "Absolutely."

"Grace, that gorgeous husband of yours is here to whisk you away again," Dora said, sticking her head into Grace's office. "Says he's here to take you to lunch."

Grace's stomach growled hungrily at the mention of food, and she smiled as she filed away the last of her invoices. Ford's impromptu visits to her shop had become a common occurrence, and something she admittedly enjoyed. Ever since the day at the cemetery almost a month ago, they'd forged a silent pact that had eased the initial strain in their relationship and enabled them to talk more openly about the past, and their new marriage, which Grace was gradually getting used to. Ford's anytime, anywhere kisses had become a delightful surprise, and she didn't even try to stop his advances. She got the impression that he was courting her, and she was helpless to resist his efforts.

She'd come to believe he'd returned to Whitaker Falls because all he wanted was acceptance, and to belong. Both were a struggle for him. Gertie and the elderly shop owners around the café were the few who didn't openly condemn Ford, and seemed willing to give him the chance he so desperately wanted to prove that he'd changed. Rallying the support of those shop owners was Gertie's doing, Grace had no doubt, but she was grateful for the other woman's advocacy.

Closing the filing cabinet, Grace glanced back at her assistant. "Do you mind me being gone for about an hour?"

Dora smiled encouragingly. "Not at all. Take two hours if you want to." She waggled her brows suggestively.

Grace rolled her eyes at her friend's insinuation. For all of the passionate kisses she and Ford had shared, and for as much as his hands roamed her body during those embraces, they'd yet to make love again. She still retired to the guest bedroom in the evenings, which was newly decorated in feminine colors and patterns. The nights were long and lonely, but Ford hadn't pressed the issue of her sharing his bed, and since her body was quickly blossoming as she neared her fourth month, she had her doubts that he'd find her pregnant state attractive and arousing.

Dismissing the depressing thought that she might not appeal to Ford in her condition, she said to Dora, "Tell him I'll be there in a minute."

When she exited her office sixty seconds later, she found her husband talking with Dora, and they were both laughing at something he'd said. He looked so handsome and relaxed, and it hit her in that moment that she was falling hopelessly in love with him all over again.

His gaze settled warmly on her from across the counter, taking in the thigh-length, multicolored shirt she'd worn over stretchy, deep purple leggings. His perusal was lazy and thorough, causing Grace's cheeks to flush. There was no hiding her growing belly, or the fact that she was, without a doubt, pregnant. When his eyes again met hers, his gaze glowed with a male pride and satisfaction that made a slow, simmering heat unfurl in the pit of her belly.

"Are you hungry?" he asked, his low, rich voice rumbling across her sensitive nerve endings.

"I'm starved," she admitted, shocked at the husky quality of her own voice.

A grin quirked his mouth, but before he could add to that, Dora leaned close to Grace and murmured, "I'm telling you, Grace, take those two hours!"

Oh, how she was tempted to give into her desire for Ford and spend the next two hours in his arms experiencing the pleasure she knew he could give her, but she didn't feel comfortable instigating something that intimate or relationship-altering.

"Would you like us to bring you back something from Gertie's?" Ford offered Dora.

"I'd love a ham and cheese on white," she said, completely charmed by Ford's polite inquiry. "And some of Gertie's potato salad would be great."

He grinned at her. "You got it."

She and Ford stepped outside, and he automatically slipped his hand into hers as they headed down the sidewalk toward the strip of run-down and cosmetically neglected shops at the far side of Whitaker Town Square. Most people had grown used to seeing the two of them together, but Ford's romantic gesture earned them a few reprehensible looks from those extremists who'd branded her a hussy behind her back, but nobody said anything to them personally. She suspected that they wouldn't dare—for all of Ford's faults, she'd come to learn that he was fiercely protective of what was *his,* and that included her and the baby she carried.

They passed the After Hours bar, and like every other time they'd walked by the disreputable establishment on their way to Gertie's, Ford's entire body tensed, but he said nothing. He didn't need to. His disgust and loathing of the place that had consumed his mother's life was evident in the enmity that sparked in his eyes.

By the time they entered Gertie's, Ford had a smile in place for the elderly woman who had treated him with kindness and consideration since he'd returned. The place was empty, except for a young teenage couple who were sharing a banana split at a table in the back. Ford led her to a booth near the window overlooking the town, and sat across from her.

Gertie ambled over with a pen and pad in hand and a smile creasing her plump, friendly face. "What can I get for my favorite newlyweds?"

Blushing at Gertie's greeting, Grace requested her usual chicken salad on rye with a side of fresh fruit and a lemonade, and also gave Gertie Dora's order. Ford opted for a cheeseburger, fries and a soda.

Gertie handed the lunch order over to her husband, Frank, who was working behind the counter, and returned a few minutes later with their drinks. Knowing the older woman was concerned about the fate of her café since the original owner of the property had died and his son, Hank, had decided to sell the property and shop structures, Grace ventured to ask, "Have you heard anything from the new property owner yet?"

"Nope," Gertie said with a frustrated sigh. "Last time I talked to Hank, he said the sale hadn't been finalized yet, and he wasn't releasing any information about the new owner until the transaction was negotiated and settled." A troubled frown etched her brows. "Hank mentioned the possibility of the new owner tearing down the original structure to build a theater and new, more modern shops."

"Oh, Gertie, no." Grace pressed a hand to her chest in dismay. Gertie and Frank depended on the café for their livelihood, as did the rest of the elderly business owners who'd operated their shops on this strip for more years than Grace had been alive. She didn't want to think about what would happen to them without the financial supplement of their businesses.

"Hard to imagine," Gertie said, a combination of umbrage and resignation lacing her voice. "But us business folks don't seem to have much say in the matter, do we?"

"Your order is up, Gert," Frank called, garnering the older woman's attention.

Grace waited while Gertie delivered her sandwich and Ford's cheeseburger, but somewhere between entering the café and being served, Grace had lost her appetite. All she could think about was all the people who would be put out of business by this entrepreneur.

"Hey, I thought you were hungry," Ford said, then took a big bite of his burger.

"I'm too upset to eat," she said, sliding her plate to the edge of the table.

He pushed the meal back in front of her. "Feed my baby," he said gently, but firmly.

She sighed in resignation, knowing he was right. She had someone other than herself to think about and couldn't withhold nutrition because of her personal worries. Picking up her fork, she stabbed it into her potato salad, too perturbed to keep her opinion on this matter quiet. "I just can't believe someone would buy this property, and tear down what's been here for so many years. These shops are as much a part of Whitaker Falls as I am."

"Times change, Grace, and so do people's needs." Picking up his soda, he took a long drink of the dark, fizzing liquid. "I have to agree that this structure of shops is getting pretty dilapidated looking, especially when you compare it to Whitaker Town Square.''

Her mouth pursed in annoyance at his calm, rational point of view of the situation. ''It doesn't matter to you that it would put so many good, honest, hardworking people out of business?''

His expression turned shrewd, and somewhat defensive. ''You can't think of it that way, but rather all the new employment opportunities it will open for others. A theater and new stores would be a good thing for the town to keep it modern and fresh, not to mention getting rid of After Hours, which just downgrades this entire strip of shops.'' The tinge of resentment in Ford's tone was unmistakable.

''That's the only thing I agree with,'' she said, taking a small bite of her sandwich and chewing. ''That place only serves to draw in a disreputable crowd and hurts the other businesses. But why should everyone be penalized for one seedy establishment?''

''It's just the way of business, Grace,'' he said, his voice uncharacteristically hard and uncompromising.

''The way of business?'' she repeated incredulously. ''To put people out of work who depend on the income of their businesses for their sole support? Most of these people have been running their shops for years and know nothing else but their business. What about them?''

Ford dragged a French fry through a pool of ketchup, his face a mask of indifference. ''Maybe it's a sign that they ought to retire.''

''Some of these folks don't have a choice but to work, and barely make ends meet as it is,'' she argued vehemently. "Tearing down these shops is as good as making them homeless."

Ford dropped his napkin on his empty plate and pushed it aside, hating the guilt pricking his conscience for the secret he was keeping. At the moment, he had no choice. FZM had made a very substantial offer on the very property he was sitting on and the businesses Grace was so staunchly supporting, but the appropriate paperwork had yet to be signed, sealed and delivered, and until he held the title in his hands, he knew better than to take the sale for granted. Considering how defensive Grace was about the store owners, and how opposed she was to the new property owner redeveloping the land, Ford realized he only had a few weeks to sway his wife to his way of thinking.

"It's just not fair," she said unhappily, her gaze on Gertie and Frank as they worked the small café.

Knowing he was the cause of her morose mood, he sought to offer some kind of comfort. "I'm sorry," he said, belatedly realizing the sentiment extended beyond this disagreement.

Her features immediately softened with her own apology, and she reached across the table, placing her hand over his. "Of course it's not your fault," she said, compounding his guilt with those oh-so-innocent words. "There's just got to be another way, some kind of compromise that would benefit the shop owners and the new property owner."

Ford's heart shriveled a little in his chest. Buying and redeveloping this property, and destroying the After Hours bar, was his way of reconciling the bitter memories of his past.

For him, there was no compromise at all.

CHAPTER EIGHT

"Close your eyes, and don't open them until I tell you to," Ford instructed.

Holding Ford's hand, Grace kept her eyes squeezed shut as she followed her husband, trusting him to guide her. She knew they were headed toward the barn and corral, but couldn't imagine what had Ford so anxious. When she'd woken up from her nap this afternoon, she'd found him in the kitchen waiting for her, his eyes bright and hopeful. He'd looked like a little kid who couldn't wait to share a new toy, and his infectious enthusiasm had bubbled over to her.

Finally, he stopped. Releasing her hand so he could stand behind her, he rested his palms lightly on her shoulders. His mouth moved near her ear, and he said in a deep voice laced with excitement, "Okay, you can look now."

She blinked her lashes open, and her breath caught in her chest as she stared at two of the most magnificent horses she'd ever seen. They stood in the corral, comfortable in their new surroundings. Their rich, healthy chestnut coats gleamed in the warm sunshine, and their dark eyes were amicable.

"Oh, Ford," she breathed in awe, overwhelmed by this latest surprise. "They're absolutely beautiful."

"The chestnut closest to us, Sophie, is yours," he

said, a pleased smile in his voice. "And that one over there is Maggie."

The one named Sophie ambled up to the fence and blew out a welcoming snort of breath. Grace laughed, delighted, and stroked a hand down her snout. "Ever since I was a little girl, I've always wanted a horse of my own."

"I'm glad I was able to give you one." Ford tucked a stray strand of hair behind her ear that had escaped her French braid. Grace suspected it was more of an excuse to touch her, but she enjoyed his caresses, and liked that soft look he got in his eyes when he looked at her.

"Thank you," she said around the tightness in her throat. Filled with an irresistible need to express her gratitude in a more heartfelt way, she pressed a hand to his chest, raised up on tiptoe and brushed her lips across his. She'd meant to be quick and chaste about her kiss of thanks, but she hadn't anticipated the yearning that swept over her the moment their mouths touched. Hadn't been prepared for the flash of wildfire that ignited beneath the surface of her skin.

Ford skimmed a hand lightly down her spine, urging her closer, but giving her enough room to object if she wanted to. She didn't. Leaning more fully into him, until the taut curve of her belly conformed to his muscular one, she tilted her head and parted her lips, and for the first time since exchanging wedding vows with Ford, she was the one who initiated a kiss.

Ford let her have free rein. He even let her set the pace, and merely followed her lead. She encouraged the slow, drugging kind of kiss he'd taught her, the

kind she liked the best, because it made her feel as
though they had the rest of their lives to indulge in
the lazy melding of lips and tongues. Incredible
pleasure spread through her, and something in her
tummy fluttered—illicit need, or her baby's first
movement, she wasn't sure.

By the time she pulled back, they were both
breathing hard.

"Wow," he murmured, a rascal grin claiming his
lips. "If I'd known that's the response I'd get, I
would have bought you a horse sooner."

Shocked at her own brazenness, she stepped from
his embrace, and cleared her throat. She returned her
attention back to Sophie, enchanted by the sweet-
natured animal. "When did you get them?"

Ford came up beside her, hooking a booted foot
on the bottom rung of the fence, and resting his arms
across the top. "They were delivered while you
were taking a nap this afternoon, which worked out
well since I wanted them to be a surprise."

"Oh, they're certainly that." She laughed lightly
as Sophie nuzzled her neck affectionately. "Can we
ride them?"

Ford's smile expressed his own enjoyment of the
moment. "That depends. I've got all the necessary
gear, but I think you need to call Dr. Chase and get
his approval to ride a horse. If he says okay, we can
take them on a nice, easy stroll."

"Then I'll call him immediately." She turned and
headed back up to the house, excited at the prospect
of riding her new mare.

Since it was Sunday, she called Dr. Chase at
home. He gave her the permission she sought, as
long as she didn't allow the horse to trot or gallop.

She was physically fit, and her pregnancy was progressing well, but the jarring motion posed too many risks. To be safe, he preferred she take the ride slow and easy.

Ford insisted that she pack a light snack while he saddled up the mares. She had no idea what he intended, but an hour later, she and Ford had made their way through the forest of trees separating Cutter Creek from her property, and were guiding the horses along the lake in front of her cottage.

"What are we doing here?" she asked, mildly curious.

He glanced over at her, his body relaxed and at ease in the saddle. "I thought you might want to check on things."

It had been at least two weeks since she'd stopped by the cottage, and she supposed it wouldn't hurt to give the house a quick walk-through to make sure everything was in order. Ford helped her down from Sophie, and while he tended to the horses, she used the key she'd stashed in the planter box next to the front door and entered the cottage. The place was stuffy from being closed up, but otherwise fine. She'd moved out all of the furnishings she'd wanted to Ford's house, and had left the bare minimum that still made the cottage livable. She'd hired a gardener to keep up the lawn and planters around the house. But for as much as she missed her cozy cottage, she was beginning to think of Ford's house as her home.

She headed back outside into the late-afternoon sunshine, the mild warmth of the September day broken up by a pleasant breeze. Ford had looped the horses' reins around a low bush, allowing them to graze contentedly without straying.

Shading her eyes from the sun, she searched for Ford, and found him standing out on the dock extending to the lake, their picnic sack in hand. She approached her husband, and frowned when she saw that a sturdy new rowboat had been tied to the dock, complete with oars.

"Where did that rowboat come from?" She glanced around, startled by the thought that someone might be hiding somewhere on her property.

"I had it delivered a few days ago," he said, a smile glimmering in his eyes.

Perplexed, she could only stare at him. "Whatever for?"

"For us to use, of course." As if she'd asked a completely ridiculous question, he slid a finger down the slope of her nose, then executed a low, gallant bow. "Sailor McCabe, at your service, ma'am."

Surprise and pleasure rippled through her. "You're taking me for a boat ride?"

"Yep." He stepped into the well-built craft, bracing his legs wide to keep the small boat from rocking. Setting the picnic sack between his feet, he reached a hand up to her. "All you have to do is relax on that blanket and feed me, and I'll do all the muscle work."

"That's an offer I find hard to refuse." Utterly charmed by his romantic gesture, she placed her fingers in Ford's and allowed him to help her into the boat. She sat down on the nice, soft blanket that had been arranged at one end of the structure, and reclined back against the hull.

After untying the rope securing them to the dock, he sat on the bench opposite her, took hold of the oars and rowed them out onto the smooth surface of the lake.

She sighed complacently, enjoying the relaxing glide of the boat upon the water, and reveling in the sight of her gorgeous, sexy husband as he worked the oars with effortless, rhythmic ease. The form-fitting polo shirt he'd worn defined the width of his broad shoulders, enabling her to indulge in the sight of those firm muscles across his chest flexing as he rowed. The sun haloed his dark, rumpled hair, and he smiled lazily at her, his own pleasure evident in his peaceful expression.

Closing her eyes, she rested her head on the rim of the boat and basked in the warmth of the sun upon her face. Before long, the tranquility of the boat ride lulled her close to slumber.

"Hey, Sleeping Beauty," Ford said, nudging her foot gently. "You already had a nap today."

"Oh, but this is absolutely wonderful." She blinked her heavy eyes open, and gave him a drowsy smile. "If I would have known what you had planned, I would have saved my nap for now."

"Uh-huh," he said, shaking his head. "This is my time with you, and as beautiful as you look sleeping, I'd like to enjoy this outing with you awake."

He thought her beautiful in her pregnant condition; her heart beat a little faster. "Flattery will get you everywhere, Mr. McCabe," she teased.

He winked at her. "I sure do hope so."

Resting her hands over her belly, she regarded him thoughtfully. "You're just full of surprises today, aren't you?"

He shrugged, the movement as fluid as his strokes with the oars. "I like to see you happy."

"I am," she said, hearing the slight reservation in her voice.

He caught it, too, and prompted, "Except for?"

"My father's stubbornness, of course," she said, disgust lacing her voice. She was beyond hoping he'd come around, not when he hadn't made the slightest effort to breach the ever-widening chasm between them. In his eyes, she'd done the unforgivable when she'd married Ford, regardless of the fact that she was offering him a rare gift in the child she carried.

"I just hate the thought of him not being a part of his grandchild's life," she said, absently stroking the swell of her belly. "He knows how much this baby means to me since I didn't think I'd ever have children of my own."

"But it's my child, too," Ford said, his simple statement holding a wealth of meaning.

"That shouldn't matter," she argued, frustrated with her father's inability to get past his grudge with Ford, which would only hurt their child in the future.

"I'm glad *you* think so."

Ford's quietly spoken words affected her deeply, forcing her to realize how much this child mattered to the man she'd married, as did her opinion of him being the father of the baby.

She swallowed the emotions rising in her throat. "Ford...I know we married for the sake of this baby, and as shocked as I was to discover I was pregnant, I don't regret anything."

He gave her a lopsided grin that produced a dimple in his cheek. "Not even me forcing you to marry me?"

"I understand your reasons," she said with quiet honesty. "You didn't want your child to grow up illegitimate, and quite frankly, neither do I."

He nodded slowly. "That's one reason."

His words implied there was more, prompting her curiosity. "And the other reason?"

He stared at her for a long moment, his gaze a warm, vivid shade of violet. "If you haven't figured that out yet, you will in time."

His vague, cryptic words settled over her, confusing her mind. He'd never said he loved her, hadn't even insinuated that his feelings for her might extend beyond the friendship and caring they'd developed since they'd gotten married. She wondered if he was possibly as uncertain as she was of revealing his emotions. There was something extremely vulnerable about being in love and not knowing how the other person felt.

"So, why did you marry David?" he asked, changing the subject to one as equally unsettling as the thoughts he'd interrupted.

The most logical answer to Ford's question would be because she'd loved David, but that hadn't been the case for her. She could fabricate all kinds of believable excuses, but she and Ford had come a long way in trusting each other since they'd married, and she wanted to keep that honesty secure.

She met Ford's gaze, who was waiting for her reply. "I married David to save my reputation. He married me because he'd always had a crush on me." The smile she summoned felt forced on her own lips. "Not a great basis for a marriage."

He continued to row, long, lazy strokes that belied the intent look that leapt into his gaze. "What do you mean, to save your reputation?"

She glanced out the side of the boat to dry land, recognizing the scenery and guessing they were a good mile and a half away from her cottage. She felt as though they were in another country altogether.

"After you left, rumor of my involvement with you spread." Catching the frown that formed on his brow, she explained, "Someone must have seen us together, and guessed at our relationship. Since my virtue was in question, my father pushed for marriage between David and me. My father was determined to salvage the family name, and my reputation, so when David proposed, I accepted." As always, she'd done the right thing, showing her father that she was a "good girl."

A large tree shaded them, and Ford stopped rowing, letting the boat glide lazily on the surface of the glossy water. "Did you love David?"

Not like the way I loved you. "I cared for him," she admitted. "But we married for all the wrong reasons, and when I couldn't get pregnant, that just put an additional strain on our relationship. After five years of trying to make the marriage work, we finally divorced. According to David's mother, he's doing well in Norfolk with his new family, so I'm happy for him."

Ford nodded solemnly. "I'm sorry you had to go through that."

She smiled, feeling close to Ford, and emotionally connected. "It all worked out for the best."

"Yeah, I suppose it did," he agreed, putting his

own spin on her words. With a reciprocating smile, he stretched the muscles that had tightened from his sitting position. "If you expect me to row all the way back to the cottage, you'd better feed me and give me the strength."

Rolling her eyes at that, she sat up on her knees and reached for the sack of goodies they'd brought along. The boat rocked gently, but Ford's wide-spread feet and solid body kept her from swaying off balance.

"Easy does it," he murmured humorously. "Or else we'll be taking a swim."

Crossing her legs in front of Ford, she spread their light fare on napkins on the blanket. She placed a slice of cheese on a cracker and lifted it to his lips. He accepted the snack while she opened a bottle of apple juice to share. Then she opened the container of sliced apples, took out a wedge, and offered it to Ford.

"Mmm, apples," he said, seemingly relishing the juicy slice she'd slipped into his mouth. "Do you know what apples remind me of?"

Oh, she knew exactly what the crisp, tart fruit reminded him of, because it reminded her, too. "What?" she asked, not wanting to be the one to bring up such a sensual memory.

His gaze glowed warmly with the recollection. "It reminds me of the day you'd stopped by my house to bring me the fresh apple pie you'd baked just for me, along with two roast beef sandwiches you'd made from your family's previous night's leftovers."

She nodded, remembering painfully well the way he'd accepted the meal graciously, his hunger pangs obviously winning over pride. His own mother hadn't bothered to shop for groceries or give him money for food—she'd spent her paychecks at After Hours after working her shift as a cocktail waitress, forgetting that she had a son starving at home.

"You found me out in that dilapidated old barn behind the house, trying to chop the beams into pieces of wood to use in the fireplace so I'd have a little warmth at night." He ate another slice of apple, savoring the taste on his tongue. "I hadn't eaten anything substantial in two days and was so hungry, not that you could have known. I ate those sandwiches and half of that pie so fast that it nearly gave me a bellyache."

She laughed at the pained look on his face, and waggled a finger at him. "I warned you to slow down."

He caught the offending digit, and held her hand. Bringing her fingers to his mouth, he kissed the tips of each. A breath sighed out of her, and she melted inside.

"I thought you were an angel for bringing me that food," he said, his voice low and husky. "All I meant to do was give you a soft kiss of thanks, but you tasted even sweeter than that apple pie, and when your lips parted on a soft sigh, I couldn't resist..."

A shudder of yearning rippled through her, making her breasts swell, and her body ache. That had been the first time they'd made love, and the event had been sensual, and tender, and so very poignant. It had been pure magic.

As if feeling that same undercurrent of need that tugged at her, he released her hand, severing the contact between them. "It's getting late," he said, gathering up the remnants of their snack. "We should head back to the cottage before it gets dark."

Within a few minutes, she was reclining against the hull again as they headed back to her place. Not wanting to dwell on what had just transpired between them, she reached her arm over the side of the boat, trailed her fingers in the cool water, and enjoyed the symmetry of Ford's strokes, and the oars sluicing through the lake.

The easy ride back to Ford's house on the horses was pleasant and companionable, and when they reached the corral, he dismounted first, then came around for her. He grasped her around her thickening waist with strong hands, she rested her palms on his shoulders, and what should have been a quick help down from Sophie changed the moment Ford lifted her. Her body slid down the length of his, and he did nothing to stop the tantalizing friction. Awareness crackled between them, and his eyes darkened to velvet.

Her fingers curled around his neck, threading through the warm strands of his hair. "I had a wonderful time today," she said, trying to still her racing pulse, trying harder to stop the heat spreading like wildfire in her veins.

He kept her hips pressed against his with the slow slide of his hands around her waist. "Yeah, me, too."

They tilted their heads at the same exact moment, she lifting up on tiptoe and him dipping low. Their breaths mingled, coalesced...became one. Soft, breathless moans of pleasure rumbled between them. The kiss they shared was a joint effort, meeting halfway, both instigating a deeper union with the touch of their tongues.

The rolling sensation in the pit of Grace's belly startled her, and she jerked back, eyes wide. "Oh," she said, splaying a hand low on her abdomen, where she'd felt the movement.

"What's wrong?" Worry roughened Ford's tone.

"I think it's the baby moving." She looked up at Ford in wonder. "I felt it earlier today, but wasn't sure. This time, I'm certain that's what the fluttering sensation was."

Without asking, he pressed his large palm to her stomach, his expression anxious and excited, but the moment had passed, and the baby wasn't cooperating on demand. He looked so disappointed, she couldn't help but smile and reassure him.

"It'll happen again," she said, too aware of his fingers gently probing her tummy.

He looked discontented, as if he'd been deprived of some great mystery. "Grace—" He cut himself off indecisively, and thrust his fingers through his hair.

She couldn't imagine what had him so frazzled. "Ford, what is it?"

He frowned at her, then finally said, "I want you to share my bed."

Startled by his direct demand, she took a step back, bumping into Sophie, who shifted away with a soft snort of indignation. As much as she wanted to experience the pleasure and closeness of making love with Ford again, Grace knew she couldn't give him her body, without giving him her heart, too. And she wouldn't do that until she had his in return.

Refusing him was more difficult than she imagined. "Ford, I know our relationship is changing, and we've grown closer the past few months, but I think it's best if we remain in separate beds for now." *Until you tell me you love me.*

He shook his head. "I'm not trying to proposition you," he said, a wry grin canting his mouth. "I want you to share my bed so I can share in the experience of you being pregnant with my baby. I find everything about you being pregnant fascinating, and it's hardly fair that you get to experience everything, and I can only imagine what it's like."

Humor bubbled within her. "I'm afraid 'imagining' is all you'll be able to do."

"I want to be a part of this pregnancy," he clarified. "I want to feel those first movements, I want to see the daily changes in your body, and I want to talk to my daughter as she grows."

"Daughter?" she repeated softly, completely beguiled by his request.

He gave a nonchalant shrug and dragged his thumb along her cheek. "I can't help it if I'd like a little girl, just as beautiful as her mother."

A huge lump formed in her throat, and her heart swelled with a multitude of emotion.

He wound a finger around a silky strand of hair, captivating her in more ways than one. "Will you move into my bedroom?"

His sweet request was more than she could resist. He wasn't demanding this time, but asking. And more than anything, she wanted to share this experience with someone else, too—and who better than her husband?

"I'll be there tonight," she promised.

* * *

Grace felt as shy and modest as a bride on her wedding night, which was ridiculous, she chastised her reflection in Ford's master bathroom mirror. She and Ford weren't going to make love—he only wanted to be close to the child she carried, something she could hardly fault.

Suppressing the jumble of nerves swarming in her belly, she tied the ribbon that held the bodice of her gown together just above her breasts. The pale pink nightgown she'd bought a few days ago flowed in a billow of cotton to her knees, where it ended with a ruffled hem. The design wasn't very flattering to her figure, leaving plenty of room for her soon-to-be burgeoning tummy. She'd selected the gown for comfort, and because the buttons down the front would allow her to use the nightie to breast-feed the baby after it was born.

She dragged a brush through her unbound hair, wishing she had something prettier to wear, then immediately shook that notion from her head. The purpose of her moving into Ford's bedroom wasn't to seduce her husband, but to give him time to bond with his baby. She could do that just as easily, and possibly more effectively, if she was wearing something unappealing.

She heard his footsteps in the adjoining master bedroom, and her heart beat faster. She spent another ten minutes making sure she'd smoothed every tangle from her hair, brushed her teeth until they were so clean they squeaked, and fussed with her unattractive gown. With no more excuses left to postpone what she'd agreed to, she drew a steady breath and stepped inside Ford's bedroom.

He was half-undressed, wearing only a warm,

sensual smile, and a pair of jeans, the first button of which was unsnapped. His shirt was gone, and so were his boots and socks. Looking away from the arousing sight of his bare chest, she headed toward the four-poster bed and pulled down the spread and covers.

"Did you get everything moved over okay?" he asked from behind her.

"Yes." She plumped the pillows unnecessarily, keeping her gaze on the task. "Your walk-in closet is huge."

"When I designed the house, I did so in hopes that I'd be sharing that closet with someone." The sound of a zipper lowering rasped in the room, then the rustle of material sliding off as he shucked his jeans.

Grace snuck a peek across the expanse of the king-size bed, relieved to find Ford wearing a pair of white briefs. Though the snug underwear left little to her imagination, it was a barrier she appreciated to keep temptation at bay.

Sliding into her side of the bed, she arranged the covers up under her arms. "I took the two empty drawers in the armoire for my lingerie," she said, trying to keep the conversation casual during what felt like such an intimate moment.

"That's fine." He joined her in the big bed, leaving the lamp on to illuminate the room. Propping himself up on his elbow, he let the sheet and blanket drape around his hips. "If you need more room, let me know."

She smiled. "Okay."

He smiled back, a lazy lifting of his lips, and crooked his finger at her. "Come closer, Grace," he said, amusement in his tone. "You're so close to the edge I'm afraid you're gonna fall off the mattress."

"I'm fine, really," she insisted lightly.

"I don't bite," he promised, laughter glimmering in his eyes. "But I do want to touch you, like we agreed. And I can't do that if there's a yard of space between us."

She could hardly argue with his logic, but couldn't stem her own timidity. "This is awkward," she said, scooting closer.

He inched over, too, meeting her halfway, until she lay right next to him and she could feel the heat of his body pressed against her side. In the process, he'd managed to slide the covers down to their knees.

"It shouldn't be." He looked down at her, his expression gentle. "You're my wife, and not only that, I've seen you naked before."

She gulped. He planned to see her *naked?* She was prepared for those hands of his to touch her, but she'd thought she'd have the protection of her gown, a layer of defense between her body and his exploring fingers and heated gaze.

He reached out and touched the ribbon that tied the bow at the bodice of her gown. She grasped his wrist before he could tug on the thin strip of satin, and he immediately stilled.

Their gazes met, his filled with patience and admirable self-control. "I want to see the changes in your body. Will you let me?"

Insecurities swamped her. She wasn't very big yet, but even she'd noticed new lush curves to her once slender body. Though she scrutinized her blossoming figure from a maternal viewpoint, and reveled in the miraculous changes, she wasn't sure how Ford would view the transformation from slim and svelte to plump and rounded.

He seemed to understand. "If I do anything you don't like, just tell me to stop and I will."

Ultimately, she knew he'd keep his word. She just wasn't sure she trusted herself when Ford's mere gaze had the ability to unravel her. How would she survive his caresses?

Forcing herself to relax, she released his wrist. He gave a gentle tug, and the ribbon unfurled, revealing a teasing glimpse of the swells of her breasts. As if he had all the time in the world, his long fingers worked at the buttons, slowly undoing them until he reached the last one, right over her rib cage.

She was still decently covered, but the anticipation of knowing what he intended caused her chest to rise and fall with rapid breaths. And still, he took his time exploring, reveling in every moment. His warm palm smoothed beneath the neckline of her open gown, gliding over her collarbone and gradually moving down. Finally, he parted the material to the side, baring one plump, blue-veined breast to his reverent gaze.

Seemingly enthralled with how full and firm she'd become, he cupped the heavy weight of her flesh in the palm of his hand. Her breast grew excruciatingly tighter in his gentle grasp, and she sucked in a startled gasp when he rasped his thumb over the velvety tip, puckering her nipple.

He immediately released her, his awed expression quickly changing to a concerned frown. "Did I hurt you?"

She shook her head, and managed a husky,

"No." Quite the contrary—his touch felt good, arousing and thrilling. "My breasts are just very sensitive."

His features relaxed again. "I'll be more careful."

Before she could reassure him that he hadn't caused her any real discomfort, she felt his fingers graze her knee, then skim up her thighs, which quivered from that light stroking. Cool air washed over her heated skin as he traveled higher, pooling the hem of her gown around his wrist as he reached her stomach. She didn't have to look down to know she was exposed to his gaze, from chest to thighs, except for the material bunched around her ribs, and her panties, which he'd inched lower so he could splay his hand over her protruding abdomen. Amazingly, his long fingers spanned her taut, curved belly, lovingly cradling the life inside her in the palm of his hand.

A profound breath shuddered out of him. "I never thought I could want something as much as I want this baby." He glanced up at her, staring deeply into her eyes. His gaze held a wealth of emotion and gratitude so powerful she felt it to her very soul. "You're giving me something I never believed I'd ever have."

She rested her hand over his, threading their fingers, joining the three of them as one. "And what's that?" she whispered.

"A family," he said, his voice tight and raspy. "Security. Laughter and love in our home."

A rush of tears stung the backs of Grace's eyes, and she managed, just barely, to keep them at bay. His words said so much, but she wanted, needed, so much more. She needed his love—not for the baby she carried that would make his life complete, but for *her,* as his wife, and the woman who loved him unconditionally.

With their hands still clasped over her belly, he leaned over her, sliding his other hand into her unbound hair to cup the back of her head. Lifting her mouth to his, he kissed her, slow and deep and luxuriously, making her weak with desire in no time flat.

Breaking the kiss, he buried his face in the curve of her neck, drawing deeply of her scent. "You smell so good," he murmured, his warm breath dampening her skin.

She felt so pliant, so dewy, all she could manage was a soft moan.

He strung a series of moist kisses along the slender column of her throat, nuzzled the curve under her jaw, touched his tongue to the pulse pattering at the base of her collarbone.

Sensual hunger coiled low and deep within her, and she shifted restlessly beside him. "Ford..." Her voice quivered with uncertainties.

"I'm only kissing you, Grace," he murmured soothingly. "And touching you."

She swallowed. Hard. She'd given him the right to kiss her, anytime, anywhere. It was the *anywhere* that concerned her at the moment...as well it should have, because his mouth glided down, and his tongue traced the slope of her breast all the way to the aching crest...which he kissed in the most delicious, sensuous way.

A whimper escaped her, and her hand lifted, clenching in his silky hair—not to push him away, but to hold him close.

"So many tastes and textures," he whispered in fascination, continuing on once he'd spent a fair amount of time lavishing attention to her breasts.

He scooted down on the bed, until finally he pressed an achingly tender kiss on the center of her belly, just below her navel, then rubbed his cheek over the taut, silky skin stretched over her abdomen. And then, as if he and the baby were the only ones present in the room, he murmured silly, nonsensical things that made Grace smile, and no doubt soothed the daughter Ford was so certain she was having.

After what seemed like an eternity of pacifying caresses over her belly and hushed secrets and promises between father and daughter, she heard Ford express his love and adoration for the child that wasn't even born yet. Grace's heart filled to overflowing at the incredibly sweet gesture, and the bond that would no doubt form between father and child over the months to come.

When he was done, Ford gathered her in his arms, tucking her back securely to his chest, and kept his hand splayed protectively over their baby. As much as Grace loved being held in Ford's embrace, she was sure if she had to endure this every night, she was going to expire from a slow, sensual death before the baby was born.

CHAPTER NINE

"GOOD afternoon, Grace," Dr. Chase acknowledged her amicably as he walked into the examination room, his head bent as he perused her prenatal chart.

Annoyance flickered through Grace, not because of anything Dr. Chase had done, but because she'd made a specific request that had obviously been blatantly disregarded.

Shutting the door behind him, Dr. Chase lifted his gaze, which settled on Ford, who'd stood up from the only armchair in the small room as soon as he'd entered.

The two men shook hands, a firm grip that bespoke of equal respect. Dr. Chase had come to the conclusion that Ford was in Whitaker Falls to stay, and had no qualms about him residing in the town where he'd grown up. Ford had been an exemplary citizen since his return, and though there were those who were holding fast to grudges, most had grown accustomed to his presence, and no longer treated him as a pariah.

"Hello, Ford," Dr. Chase said pleasantly, adjusting his glasses on the bridge of his nose. "I'm glad you could make it to the appointment today."

Ford's chest all but puffed out in pride. "I'll be here for every appointment until the baby is born."

The doctor nodded his approval. "That's great. It's nice to see a father take an active role in the baby's gestational period.'' Setting her chart on the side counter, he took a pen from his pocket to write notes, keeping his back to Grace. "So, how are you feeling, Grace?"

Grace's fingers curled into the edge of the examination table, her irritation mounting. Dr. Chase was avoiding eye contact with her, for a very good reason. "Just fine."

"Good." He kept his head bent over her chart. "Are you experiencing any abnormal discomforts that might concern you?"

Just the need to scream in frustration. "No."

"You only gained two pounds this past month, and your blood pressure looks excellent," he said, commenting on the statistics Marcie had taken before leading her to the examination room.

Tired of avoiding an issue she knew full well he was aware of, she called him on it. "Dr. Chase, I requested that my father be present at this appointment. We're supposed to hear the baby's heartbeat, and I wanted him to be here."

Finally, he turned and looked at her, a silent apology etching his features. "He asked me to handle today's checkup when Marcie mentioned that Ford was here."

Grace didn't think her father's blatant rejection could hurt so badly, but it did. She shouldn't have been surprised that her father had refused to see her once he'd discovered Ford was present, but hearing the baby's heartbeat was something she wanted to share with both her husband, and her father. She'd foolishly hoped that the first auditory confirmation of the child she carried would somehow, someway, soften the resentment Ellis Holbrook had cloaked himself in for eleven years.

"Is he here?" she asked pointedly.

Dr. Chase appeared extremely uncomfortable under her scrutiny. Very reluctantly, he admitted, "Yes, he's in his office."

"Fine." Her tone was firm, and sounded much more confident than she felt. "Then I'll speak to him after we're done, without you or Marcie warning him beforehand."

Dr. Chase didn't look happy about that, but issued no argument. Ford said nothing, either—he knew how important it was to her to reach some kind of compromise with her father, and though he was the cause of their rift, Ford had promised her she'd have his full support, always. So far, he'd been true to his word.

Now that Grace's confrontation had dispelled the awkwardness between her and the doctor, he continued with the checkup. Ford asked more questions than she did, and when Dr. Chase finally found her baby's heartbeat with the fetal monitor and they all heard that clear, powerful, *chug, chug, chug,* echoing in the room, Grace knew the pure, unadulterated joy on Ford's face was something she would remember for the rest of her life.

The precious moment warmed Grace, but her happiness was eclipsed by the surprise meeting she'd planned for her father. Somehow, Ford and Dr. Chase had detoured into a discussion about quarter horses, which Dr. Chase's father had bred and raised years ago. While the two men debated bloodlines, Grace slipped from the examination room and headed down the hall to her father's private office.

The door was closed, and she didn't bother to knock, not wanting to give her father the opportunity to refuse her.

She found him sitting behind his large mahogany desk, his reading glasses perched on his nose as he read the file in his hand. He frowned at her for barging into his private domain and interrupting him, but he didn't issue an objection.

He set the report on his desk, his gaze remaining on her face. "Is everything okay?" he asked, his tone gruff.

She approached his desk, hating that he looked so tired and haggard, beaten even—more so than she could ever remember. "Do you really care if everything is okay?" It was an honest question, and she wanted an equally honest answer.

"Of course I care about you," he replied indignantly.

He cared about *her,* but not the baby she carried. *Ford's* baby. That much was clear in his words, and the way he avoided looking at her growing tummy, evident beneath the maternity blouse she'd worn.

"Your grandchild has a strong, healthy heartbeat," she said, hoping that bit of news would soften him, along with the use of the word "grandchild."

His gaze grew hard, concealing the glimpse of misery she'd seen in his eyes. "I don't have a grandchild," he said coolly.

She flinched at his callous words. Her mind registered that he was speaking out of pain and old resentments, but her heart felt as though he'd just trampled on it. "This baby is a part of you, too, Dad," she said, ruthless in her attempt to make him see reason. "And it's a part of Mom and Aaron, as well."

"That baby is *Ford's*," he spat bitterly. "This child will only remind me of everything I lost because of him, including you!"

His anguish was so palpable, she wanted to cry. Indeed, tears stung the backs of her eyes. "Oh, Dad, you haven't lost me," she said in a tight, aching voice. "I'm right here, if you'd only let me be a part of your life again."

Need warred with uncompromising emotions in his gaze. "So long as you stay married to him, I can't." As if that were the final say on the matter, he picked up the file on his desk and opened it to read, dismissing her.

A tear trickled out of the corner of her eye, and she swiped it away, angry at her father's stubbornness, and so torn and confused over her growing feelings for Ford, and the possibility of losing her father forever. How could she choose between the two most important men in her life?

With a deep, shuddering breath, she headed for the office door, but turned back around before exiting, catching her father watching her, his expression tormented.

"It doesn't have to be this way, Dad," she said, holding her head high in an attempt to appear composed when she was falling apart inside. "This child and I are the only family you have. I love you, and I want this child to be a part of your life, as it should be, but the choice is ultimately yours."

Then she left, leaving the future of his grandchild, and his part in the child's life, up to him.

* * *

"It just isn't fair," Dora complained as she glanced across the workbench at Grace, where they were each finishing up a bouquet—one for Reverend Jones's wife for their fortieth anniversary, and another for Marvel Huff's eighty-third birthday. "You absolutely, positively, glow these days."

Grace grinned, and thought, *It's because I'm absolutely, positively, in love with my husband.* She was all but bursting with the emotion, but kept the comment to herself since she'd yet to let Ford in on the revelation.

"Pregnancy does wonders for your skin," Grace said, attaching a big, fat, pink bow to Marvel's floral arrangement and finishing it off. "And for once in my life, my nails are all the same length and no longer brittle, thanks to those prenatal vitamins I have to take. My hair feels healthier, too."

"Amazing," Dora said, trimming the stem of a dark red snapdragon. "I suppose having a gorgeous husband who dotes on you is the reason for that sparkle in your eyes and your bubbly personality lately."

"Yeah, he is," she admitted, refusing to deny what was so blatantly obvious.

Despite her rocky relationship with her father, her husband and marriage couldn't be more wonderful. She enjoyed Ford's company immensely, and hated when they were apart—by the end of the workday she was anxious to see him, and be with him. They spent the evenings together in his big bed, talking about the past, and the future, and sealing a bond between her, him, and the baby that would make them a family.

The only thing missing from their flourishing

marriage was the kind of wondrous, physical intimacy husbands and wives shared. True to Ford's word, he didn't press her to make love, but the exquisite pleasure he lavished on her with his exciting kisses and thrilling caresses as he familiarized himself with her blossoming curves was nothing short of torment.

For the past week she'd been gathering up the nerve to reveal her feelings to Ford, hoping that he might return the sentiment and they could take the next step in making their marriage real, physically as well as emotionally. She craved a deeper union, and knew he did, too. She was ready to be Ford's wife, in every sense of the word, but she was still working up the courage to lay her deepest feelings bare.

Carrying her cheerful bouquet of spring flowers to the refrigerator, she wondered if tonight might be a good time to plan a romantic dinner, and let things progress from there. Ford had called a little over an hour ago, promising to be home from his meeting in Richmond by six. That gave her four hours to stop at the market and run by Gertie's for the chocolate cream pie that Ford liked. And maybe she'd see what Shalimar's had in the way of a pretty, silky nightgown to complement her fuller figure.

Pleased with her plan, she grabbed a cellophane-wrapped spray of hyacinths, deep purple anemones and English ivy, and stepped from the unit. "I think I'll take Gertie some flowers."

Dora lifted a knowing brow. "Ah, You're craving a banana-cherry chocolate milkshake, aren't you?"

The mention of the ice-cream treat she'd come to favor did make her stomach grumble. "Are you saying I have ulterior motives for visiting Gertie and giving her flowers?''

Dora nodded and laughed. ''Let's just say that lately you've been making daily trips to the café for that odd delicacy.''

Her chin lifted in mock defense. ''It's not odd.''

Dora rolled her eyes. ''Only a pregnant woman wouldn't think so.''

Grace made a face at her assistant and went to retrieve her purse from the office. A few minutes later she headed out the door, saying hello to Patty Goldberg as she entered Grace and Charm to place an order. The brief lull in business had ebbed, as had the animosity toward Ford—except for her father's resentment, which was something Grace refused to dwell on at present.

At the moment, life couldn't be more perfect. She was determined that tonight with Ford would be equally flawless.

''You here for your afternoon banana-cherry chocolate milkshake?'' Gertie's tone was friendly enough, but her gaze lacked its normal cheerful sparkle.

Grace grinned impishly at the other woman, who stood on the opposite side of the long counter separating the dining area from the grill. ''Boy, am I predictable, or what? I also need a whole chocolate cream pie to go.'' Hoping to put a smile on Gertie's too serious expression, she extended the bouquet of flowers. ''And I brought you some flowers to brighten your day.''

Her eyes softened at the thoughtful gesture, but didn't ease the troubled frown creasing her brow. ''I certainly needed that today.'' Reaching beneath the counter, Gertie withdrew one of the expensive crystal vases Grace had given her from all those roses Ford had bought her. "Would you mind putting the flowers in water while I make your milkshake?''

Grace filled the vase with water from behind the counter, then set about arranging the spray of flowers while Gertie blended her concoction of bananas, cherries, chocolate syrup and vanilla ice cream. Grace snuck surreptitious glances at the older woman, wondering what had her so preoccupied. Gertie was never this quiet unless something was wrong.

Pouring the mixture into a tall glass, she set it in front of Grace. "Here you go, sweetie-pie.''

The silly sentiment lacked its normal *oomph*, prompting even more concern from Grace. "Gertie…is everything okay?''

Reaching inside the glass enclosed refrigerator displaying the half-dozen pies and cakes Gertie made, she retrieved one of the chocolate cream pies and slid it into a bakery box, her back to Grace. "I got an interesting call from Hank today.''

"Oh,'' Grace breathed in understanding, her hands stilling on a stem of English ivy. "Did you find out who the new property owner is?''

"Sure did.'' Her tone was calm, but undeniably disturbed as she taped the sides of the bakery box. "Title was transferred today, along with confirmation from Hank that we'll be out of business within the next two months in lieu of a new theater and shopping center.''

Grace's heart plummeted at that devastating news. "Oh, Gertie… Maybe we can contact whoever it is, and try to talk to them. See if we can't work something out that would benefit them and the tenants here.''

Gertie finally turned around, placing the dessert on the counter. Her gaze held Grace's steadily. ''You can talk to him this evening, I'm sure.''

Sure she'd misunderstood the other woman, Grace shook her head. ''Excuse me?''

Gertie washed her hands and dried them on a terry towel. ''FZM, Inc., isn't that the development company that bought Cutter Creek? The same business Ford owns?''

A numbing sensation spread within Grace, and she had to sit down on the stool next to her. ''Yes.''

A sad smile touched Gertie's mouth. ''Well, then, it looks like your husband is going to be our new landlord until he tears the place down.''

''That's impossible, Gertie,'' Grace said in fierce denial, refusing to believe it could be true. ''Ford knows how I feel about whoever is planning to redevelop this property.''

Surprisingly, Gertie expressed no anger, just resignation at the twist fate had delivered. ''Which is probably why he hasn't said anything to you.''

Ford parked his car next to Grace's van in the driveway and drew a deep breath, knowing the time had come for him to tell Grace about his recent acquisition, which would change the future of Whitaker Falls. The property and building that housed After Hours and the strip of shops was finally his, to do as he pleased. *To make peace with his past.*

Now he just needed to convince Grace that his idea for the piece of land was viable, and beneficial to the town. He needed her to understand how important this was to him, and how much he wanted her support in his new endeavor to tear down the existing structure and rebuild a theater and new, modernized shops. Destroying After Hours was his main goal, but in the process he wanted to offer Whitaker Falls something that would appeal to all.

Considering how staunchly Grace defended the current tenants, he had his doubts about her empathizing with his point of view of the situation, even if they had come a long way in their marriage. He'd spent the past few months cultivating her faith in him, needing her to believe in him, and stand behind him, for what he planned to propose.

Unfortunately, he wasn't sure he was prepared to reveal his intentions, and he wasn't so certain Grace was ready to accept them.

Frustration tightened the muscles across his shoulders. He needed more time to sway her to his way of thinking. He had at least another week before he sent letters to the tenants of the building and informed them of his plans for the property, which gave him another week to discuss the issue with Grace, and most importantly, to do the one thing he'd put off for far too long.

He needed to tell Grace he loved her, and make her confident in his feelings for her. He'd held back on the vulnerable emotions, so uncertain of where he stood with her, other than the obvious reason that had brought them together: their baby. Tonight, he planned to find out. And from there, they'd work together to solidify their future, and that of Whitaker Falls.

Satisfied with his plan, he grabbed his briefcase

and exited the vehicle, heading up the brick pathway to the front door. He stepped inside, saw the two suitcases sitting in the foyer and couldn't stem the foreboding that slithered through him…couldn't quash the sudden intuition that the week he'd thought he'd had had just been squeezed into nonexistence.

Refusing to think the worst until he had an explanation for that luggage, he set his briefcase on the dining-room table, and followed the rustling sounds he heard to his master bedroom. Sure enough, his wife was packing all her personal belongings, stuffing them haphazardly into the handled bags on the bed.

He leaned against the doorjamb and forced a calm he was far from feeling. "Are you going somewhere?"

Her body tensed at the sound of his voice, but she didn't look at him. "I'm moving out."

The pressure in his chest increased. "May I ask why?"

She cast him a quick glance as she marched to the armoire to gather her things from a drawer. The contempt in her gaze cut sharper than a knife. "You shouldn't have to ask why," she said, her tone just as double-edged. "But since you feel the need for me to clarify my reasons, I refuse to live with a man I don't trust."

He found her statement too ambiguous, and until he knew exactly what she was referring to, he decided to abstain from revealing anything. Pushing off the doorjamb, he entered the bedroom, and stopped next to the bed. "What are you talking about?"

A disgusted sound slipped past her lips. "I'm talking about the fact that *you're* the one who bought the After Hours property, Ford."

He felt as though he'd been punched in the gut, and tried not to let his unease show. He had to remain calm and rational, though he was feeling anything but. "How did you find out?"

"Does it matter?" she asked, her voice high and incredulous.

"Yes, it does," he insisted, unable to temper the irritable emotions touching his voice. "Especially when *I* wanted to be the one to tell you."

"Hank called and told Gertie today, not that that changes anything." She pushed a handful of socks and panties into the bag, and zipped it up with awful finality. Then she turned to look at him with accusing brown eyes. "You lied to me."

He shoved his hands deep into the pockets of his trousers, trying to hold on to the calm that seemed to be deteriorating by the minute. "I never lied."

"You omitted the truth, which is something you're pretty good at doing." The soft lips he'd kissed so ardently just the night before, in this very bed, were now drawn into a tight line. "You acted as though you knew nothing when we sat in Gertie's Café and talked about what the new owner might do to that property! To me, that's as good as lying, just like you *omitted* the fact that you were moving to Cutter Creek that first day I saw you."

He ground his teeth to tamp his growing aggravation. "That's not fair."

"It's not fair to *me*, Ford," she argued, picking up the two handled bags. "I'm your wife, and I didn't have the slightest clue what you'd planned. I feel deceived and betrayed by my own husband.''

He grabbed the totes from her grasp in an attempt to relieve her of the burden, and to keep her from leaving. ''I had reasons for waiting to tell you about me buying the land. I wasn't even sure I'd get the property.''

''Well, congratulations, Mr. McCabe, it's yours,'' she said sarcastically, granting him no leniency. Seemingly not caring whether she had the bags he held in his hands, or not, she turned on her heel and headed out the door.

Ford panicked. ''Grace!'' he called after her, even though he knew his obstinate wife wouldn't come running back at his demand. ''Aw, hell,'' he muttered, and dropped her bags on the floor so he could stalk after her. He caught up with Grace in the foyer, stepping between her and the luggage waiting there to be picked up.

''Dammit, Grace, I'm not done talking to you!''

Instead of the anger he'd expected, she looked up at him with a wealth of disillusionment shimmering in her eyes. ''Just be honest with me about one thing, Ford. You're tearing down those shops, *all of them,* aren't you?''

''Yes, I am,'' he said, hating how ruthless he sounded. But that's how he felt about his reasons for purchasing that property in the first place. ''Those shops are old, and I want After Hours gone. Even you agree that the bar is an eyesore.''

Her brows snapped into a scowl. ''I don't want After Hours torn down at the expense of putting other good, honest, hardworking people out of business because of your selfish ideas!''

His jaw firmed. "I can't do it any other way."

"Can't, or won't?"

The past rose up to haunt him, brooking no compromise. "I *can't,* Grace."

"Well, I can't do it any other way, either." Her expression saddened. "I can't live with a man I don't even know. A man who won't even confide in me for the most important decisions in his life. I thought we'd come at least that far in this farce of a marriage." She attempted to step around him to pick up her luggage.

He blocked her path, but didn't touch her, though he wanted to. Badly. "Our marriage was never a farce."

"Wasn't it?" she insisted, vulnerable emotions trembling in her voice. "You married me because I was pregnant with your baby, and now I see everything for the sham it is. You moved back to Cutter Creek to prove something, and you've certainly created a nice illusion for yourself, with a sprawling house, a wife, a baby, a family. You've come a long way since the wild, rebellious kid you were, and I'm just an asset in your life to make you look respectable."

He sucked in a sharp breath. "Dammit, Grace, that's the furthest thing from the truth!" She didn't look at all convinced that his motives toward her had been emotion-driven. Desperation coiled through him, and instinctive words blurted from him. "*I love you,* and I don't want you to leave!"

She nearly unraveled at his declaration—he saw the softening in her gaze, the wonderment of the possibility that what he said was true. But then the moment was gone and she gave her head an imperceptible shake. "You've given me no choice but to leave, because I can't even be sure if you really love me, or if you're using my emotions to get what you want."

"Which is?"

"My cooperation. My approval." Her chin jutted out mutinously. "You want me to stand by you in your decision to tear down all those shops, but I can't do that, Ford. I care for those people who've worked hard all their lives and won't have a means for income any longer. You're destroying more than those shops, Ford, you'll be destroying people's dreams at the expense of exorcizing your own demons." She pulled in a shaky breath, the briefest hint of compassion entering her eyes. "Tearing down After Hours and rebuilding something new won't make the pain of your past go away, or give you what you want so badly."

The only thing he wanted so badly at the moment was her. Nothing else. But he didn't know how to breach the ever-widening chasm between them, didn't know how to shake the defensive emotions that gripped him inside.

Tears filled her eyes, but she valiantly blinked them back. "If you want to be respected and accepted in this community, then you need to do something *respectable.* And until you figure out a way to do that, I'll be living at the cottage."

His hands clenched into fists at his side. "You're my wife, Grace," he said, emotions harshening the tone of his voice. "And I want you here, where you belong."

"And you're my husband, Ford, and I need to trust you," she whispered as one fat tear spilled out of the corner of her eye and trickled down her cheek. "Right now, I don't."

This time, when she stepped around him, he let her go, knowing there was nothing else he could say or do to stop her from leaving.

As he heard the front door close softly behind her, he was struck with the realization that for all he'd gained, he'd just lost the single-most important thing in his life.

His wife.

CHAPTER TEN

FORD scrubbed a hand down his face, feeling the burn of a two-day stubble against his palm. It had been that long since Grace had left him, and he'd spent both days holed up in his office at the back of the house, spending his time taking calls from his estimator who worked out of the office in Richmond, and poring over the proposed plans he'd developed for the property he'd coveted.

The land was now his. He thought he'd feel vindicated somehow, since one of the establishments on that property was the cause of so many awful memories for him. But his triumph was overshadowed by the parting comment Grace had made to him. *If you want to be respected and accepted in this community, then you need to do something respectable.*

Her words haunted him, as did the thought of losing Grace forever.

He stared at the blueprints spread out on his drafting table in front of him. Two months ago, he'd been pleased with the design and layout of the new structure he'd planned to build in town, envisioning so many opportunities for new businesses and jobs in Whitaker Falls. He'd been optimistic, and so very hopeful that his plans would appeal to the vast majority of the community. Now, he saw his ideas through Grace's eyes, the demolishing of thriving businesses, and destroying the livelihood of so many people who'd worked hard to gain security for themselves, and their families.

All these years he'd thought only of himself, and what he'd gain with this acquisition—peace, and closure to a haunting past. Buying the property had been a personal decision, as well as a business one, but he was struggling with a compromise that would benefit the businesses already established on the property, and his own internal goals.

He wanted After Hours gone, wanted to tear down the ramshackle bar that had sucked the life out of his mother, which in turn had destroyed his youth. He couldn't offer a concession on that issue, but as he spent another two hours perusing the blueprints that sketched out the theater he'd planned to build, along with over a dozen other modern shops, he came to the conclusion that there was no reason why the other businesses had to suffer the same fate.

An idea formed in his mind, a *respectable* proposition certain to appeal to all parties involved. But first, he needed to make changes to the blueprints, then he needed a sketched rendition of what he had in mind so there would be no misconstruing what he intended.

With a glimmer of excitement, he picked up the phone and dialed the number of the architect who'd originally designed the new structure. Hopefully, by the end of the following week he'd have the respect of the town, and his wife back at home where she belonged.

"Why do you suppose Ford is calling a meeting here at Whitaker Town Square?" Dora asked, peering out Grace and Charm's front windows to the crowd gathering in front of the small platform set up in the middle of the plaza.

The ache in Grace's heart that she'd been carrying with her for almost two weeks, since the day she'd left Ford, increased in pressure. "I'm sure he's going to let everyone know what he plans to do with the property that's now his."

Dora gave her a pained look. "Let's hope the crowd doesn't decide to lynch him."

Looking out at the sea of angry faces waiting for Ford to arrive, Grace could only nod in agreement. She presumed this formal gathering was Ford's way of confirming the rumors that had been circulating about his agenda to tear down the entire structure, and to build a new center. That bit of speculation had been met with open hostility and opposition, not that Ford had been around to endure the town's animosity. He'd been smart, and had kept himself scarce. Indeed, he hadn't even made any effort to contact her, which only confirmed that he intended to follow through with his original plans.

The realization caused a wave of misery to well up in her throat.

The flyers that had been distributed to every home and business in Whitaker Falls had certainly done their job in drawing out the citizens of the town. A few hundred people packed the courtyard, and the crowd was beginning to get restless.

Grace glanced at her wristwatch, which revealed there was only five minutes to go until the meeting started. She released a sigh of resignation. "I guess we should go join them and see what he has to say."

Dora nodded solemnly. Together, they walked outside, standing at the very back of the assemblage. Right on time, Ford arrived, stepping from his car with a large, thick presentation board in his hands.

He made his way up to the platform and set the board on the easel sitting next to the podium.

The upset congregation had no qualms about expressing their displeasure to the man they believed would destroy a part of their town for his own gain, and Grace couldn't blame them for being so irate, because she was equally so. Everyone knew she was opposed to Ford's plans, that she supported the tenants' rights to keep their businesses.

He tapped on the microphone to quiet down the buzz of conversation filtering through the crowd. He appeared nervous standing in front of so many incensed people, but there was also a quiet confidence about him that made Grace wonder what he intended.

"Before you start jumping to conclusions that aren't necessarily true, I want you all to hear me out, until the end." His voice was strong, and polished, exhibiting just how far he'd come from the underprivileged kid he'd been. "First off, I do want to clarify that my company, FZM, Inc. is now the new property owner of the strip of stores that used to belong to Hank's father."

Grumbling and grousing could be heard from some of the crowd, but overall everyone listened intently to Ford, wanting to hear what he had to say.

His gaze scanned the audience as if searching for someone—*her?* Grace wondered—but he remained focused on his speech. "When I first made the decision to return to Whitaker Falls, I did so for the sole purpose of returning where my roots are. I'd grown up here, and my grandfather owned Cutter Creek, which should have been mine. Things didn't work out the way I'd hoped as a kid, but then I wasn't given the chance to absolve myself of the stigma I'd lived with all my life." There was no bitterness in his tone, just a statement of fact. "I wanted to come back to Whitaker Falls and make a difference in this town."

"By putting people out of business?" A deep male voice hollered angrily from the crowd.

"What I'm proposing won't put the main establishments out of business," he said, bracing his hands on the podium. "If anything, what I've decided to do should draw more attention to those existing businesses, and help them out."

Grace noticed that Ford had certainly piqued everyone's interest, including hers.

"I'd like to take a poll, if I could." Again, his gaze searched the hundreds of faces peering up at him. "How many of you want After Hours to remain in this town?"

The only hands that raised were the few patrons that frequented the disreputable establishment, which seemed to please Ford. The vote was clearly on his side, and he took advantage of it.

"I'm tearing down After Hours," he told the residents of Whitaker Falls, and wasn't met with much protest on that issue. "And in its place I'm building a new ten-cinema theater, and a steakhouse with a lounge and dance floor, to replace After Hours."

Excited murmurs rippled throughout the throng of people, and Dora said to Grace, "You have to admit that Whitaker Falls could use a new theater and restaurant, not to mention the employment opportunities those new businesses would offer people."

Grace nodded their agreement.

"What about the other businesses that are presently there?'' someone spoke up, asking the question that had been lingering in Grace's mind. The fate of those other shops, after all, was the main concern of so many.

"As for the other establishments that are currently on that strip, I'll be giving them a structural facelift to match the new architecture of the FZM Center." Moving to the easel next to the podium, he turned the presentation board around, which revealed a preliminary sketch depicting a modernized building including the proposed theater and restaurant, and noting the existing shops in bold, black type. "All the shops will be able to remain open during renovations, so no one should lose any business."

The general consensus of the audience was support for Ford's presentation, and gratitude for his ingenuity and consideration. A sense of pride filled Grace, that her husband had managed to strike a balance between what he'd wanted, and what was in the town's best interest.

"You're a good man, Ford McCabe!''

Grace recognized the voice as Gertie's, though she couldn't see the woman in the swarm of people in front of her. Up on the platform, Ford's expression softened and he smiled. Grace wondered if he realized in that moment that he'd gained the acceptance and respect he'd craved for so long.

Gradually, like a slow rolling wave, everyone started to clap, the resounding applause echoing Gertie's approval. With tears filling Grace's eyes, and emotions crowding her chest, she made her way through the attendees and up to Ford on the platform. He watched her as she approached, his gaze hopeful, his expression so achingly vulnerable that she *knew* this man she'd adored for so long had finally made peace with his past, and was ready to embrace the future awaiting him.

He didn't care that everyone witnessed this very sentimental moment between them, and his tenderness endeared him to her even more. She stood less than a foot away from him, and though they were surrounded by hundreds of people, for her the world had narrowed down to just the two of them.

"Thank you," she said, the two simple words holding an abundance of meaning. That simple statement expressed her appreciation for the admirable man he'd become, for making respectable choices, and mostly for sacrificing something so important to him, yet gaining so much more as a result.

He understood. "I did it for you, as much as I did it for us, and our daughter."

Certain she couldn't contain the overwhelming emotions bubbling up in her, she threw herself into his arms, wrapping them both in a fierce hug.

"Don't believe a word he says about that piece of property he bought!" Grace's father's angry voice intruded on the private moment, shattering it.

Ford let her go, and she found her father out in the crowd instantly because everyone else had turned to look at Ellis Holbrook, making him the center of attention. His face was red with fury, his features creased with loathing. And all that live, seething energy was directed at Ford.

"He's only telling you what you want to hear," Ellis went on, taking advantage of the quiet that had settled in the courtyard. "Don't you remember what he did to this town eleven years ago? He destroyed lives, and he'll do it again.''

Nobody said anything, though the shocked expressions Grace saw on various faces spoke volumes. An awful premonition swirled through Grace, that her father was out to extract his own brand of vengeance toward Ford, and she couldn't allow him to disgrace himself, or the respectable man Ford had become.

She stepped forward, toward the microphone, but Ford gently grabbed her arm and stopped her. "Let him say what he needs to say, Grace.''

Ellis's expression twisted with malevolence. "You killed my son and tore apart my family, Ford McCabe! I lost everything because of you, including my daughter!'' He was so filled with rage, he nearly shook with it. "You might be making nice with the rest of the town, but you'll never be anything more than the selfish, good-for-nothing kid who never thought of anyone or anything but yourself!''

Still, Ford said nothing, just stood there with his head held high while Ellis spewed his bitter emotions. But Grace couldn't take any more, and when her father continued to publicly malign Ford's character, she *had* to put a stop to his ranting.

"That's enough,'' she said, her harsh words cutting off her father's tirade. "You're being unfair, Dad. Ford is good and honest, and he's trying to do something honorable. You have to put the past to rest, Dad, if not for me, then for your grandchild's sake.''

Just like that day in his office, he didn't seem swayed. His eyes remained dark and impenetrable.

Knowing she had nothing left to lose, she put her

heart on her sleeve for all to see. "I love you, Dad, but I love Ford, too," she said in a clear, strong voice. Her public declaration of her feelings for Ford set off a few surprised comments, but no one publicly scorned her or Ford. In fact, as she looked out at the audience, she realized she and Ford had the support of the very people who'd once ostracized him.

As for Ford, she had no idea how he'd reacted to her spontaneous announcement, since he stood behind her. She knew she should have saved her declaration for a more private moment, but she needed to make her father understand how much her marriage, and her husband, meant to her.

With her gaze, she implored him to soften, to try to find it within himself to forgive Ford for the past. "I don't want to choose between the two of you, Dad."

Ellis's glare encompassed her, then Ford. "Seems to me you've already made your choice," he said, then turned and stalked away.

Ford was furious with Grace's father—not because Ellis had humiliated him in front of the entire town, but that he'd openly rejected his own daughter. As he led Grace off the platform, his heart wrenched at the devastation reflecting on her face, and the tears of despair swimming in her eyes.

"Oh, Ford, what am I going to do?" she asked, looking to him for the answer.

Not knowing what to say, he drew her into his arms and kissed her temple, wanting nothing more than to shelter her, protect her, and take away the pain her own father had inflicted upon her. But, as he stroked her back and offered her silent comfort, he realized *he* was the wedge that had come between father and daughter, and until that chasm was somehow breached, there would always be an underlying strain to their marriage.

He loved Grace, more than he thought he could ever love another person, and it was that pure emotion that urged him to make amends with the man who'd hated him for too long.

Instead of taking Grace home, he drove to her father's two-story Victorian home. She instantly became uneasy when he parked his vehicle at the curb and cut the engine.

She caught her bottom lip between her teeth and worried it. "Ford, I don't think coming here is a good idea right now."

There would never be a better time to confront Ellis with the past than the present, he thought. He brushed his fingers along her soft cheek, trying to reassure her with that gentle touch. "There are a few things I need to say to your father, and I want you with me when I do." When she continued to look skeptical, he offered her a lopsided smile. "How much worse can it get than what we just went through?"

"Not much, I suppose," she admitted.

"Then come with me."

To his relief, she did. They exited the car and walked up the cobblestone pathway to the porch. The door was locked, and instead of alerting her father to their presence and risk him refusing them, Grace dug her key from her purse and let them in. The house was quiet, but Grace seemingly had an idea where her father might be.

They found him in the study at the back of the house, his back to the door as he looked at the framed picture of his wife in his hands.

"Ellis?" Ford said quietly.

Ellis whirled around, his gaze narrowing on Ford. The older man looked torn and tormented, and oddly enough, it made him seem very human and vulnerable. "What are you doing here?" he demanded.

Ford entered the room without being invited, with Grace beside him. She took a seat in one of the leather chairs in front of her father's desk, but Ford opted to stand.

"I think you and I have unfinished business to settle."

"I have nothing left to say to you, McCabe." Ellis set the photograph back on his desk, his gaze flickering briefly to Grace. "You know how I feel about you, your marriage to my daughter, and you trying to save face with the town."

"But you have no idea how I feel about what happened to Aaron."

"Guilt is a powerful emotion," Ellis said, his lip curling into a sneer. "Is that the reason for your return, and everything else you're doing? To shake off the guilt that's been riding you for the past eleven years?"

"No," Ford said calmly, refusing to rise to the older man's bait. He understood that Ellis was hurt and lashing out, because he'd lived that anguish himself for the past eleven years. "I used to feel guilty about what happened to Aaron, but the truth is, it was an unfortunate accident, and I just happened to be the one driving the car. I can't tell you how many nights I laid in bed, wishing it was me that died instead, but it didn't happen that way, so I've learned to forgive myself."

"How convenient."

"For me, it was a matter of self-preservation, or the guilt *would have* destroyed me. So I understand your pain, because I still live with it, too."

The defensive scowl they'd been greeted with had turned into a considering frown as Ellis listened to Ford.

"I'm sorry that you lost your son, Ellis, but I lost one of the best friends I ever had. Aaron was one of the few who befriended me at a point in my life that had become very bleak. Your son had a big heart, and so does your daughter. You ought to be proud of both of them for having such generous qualities. I plan to raise our children the exact same way."

Ellis's eyes shimmered with a multitude of emotions, and the tense set of his shoulders eased. He looked as though he were teetering between giving in and clinging to old resentments.

Ford continued, determined to reach the older man. "I know I'm not your choice for a husband for Grace, but I love her more than anything. I would never purposely hurt her, and I'm going to do everything in my power to make her happy and bring my child up in a secure, wholesome environment." That was a vow he'd keep until the end of time. "And I know I speak for the both of us when I say we'd really like for you to be a part of our family."

Ford heard Grace sniffle, and both men looked at the woman who meant so much to them.

Standing, she rounded the desk toward Ellis, her

gaze issuing the silent plea she put into words.
"Give Ford a chance, Dad," Grace whispered, rest-
ing a hand lightly over the swell of her belly.
"Please?"

His gaze dropped to the baby she carried, his expression miserable, and filled with regret. "Dammit,
Grace, I don't want to lose you!"

"You haven't." She swallowed back the tears
making her voice quiver. "You never will. I promise."

"I...I want to be a part of my grandbaby's life,"
he said, the admission seemingly costing the proud
man, yet giving him a sense of peace, too.

"That's the way it should be," Ford said, and in
a gesture meant to heal the past and pave the way
to a smooth future, he extended his hand toward
Ellis Holbrook.

Ellis hesitated for only a moment before slipping
his palm into Ford's and shaking his hand. They still
had a long way to go in becoming friends, but Ford
was optimistic that this was the first step in dissolving the dissension between them.

"Did you mean what you said today, about loving
me?"

Back at Ford's house, Grace wrapped her arms
around her husband's neck and gazed lovingly into
his violet-hued eyes. In the depth of his gaze she
saw his devotion for her, and also the barest hint of
insecurity.

She catered to the latter, knowing she was going
to spend the rest of her life making sure he knew
just how much she adored him. "Yes, I meant what

I said. I love you, Ford McCabe. And I'm sorry for doubting you.''

His large hands skimmed down her spine, warming her, and sparking a tantalizing hunger that made her breasts swell against his chest. "And I'm sorry for not telling you about me buying that property, and I hereby solemnly swear to never keep anything from you ever again.''

Her fingers threaded through the soft hair at his nape as the awareness between them increased. "All you have to do is trust me, Ford, and I'll give you the same in return.''

A smile eased up the corners of his mouth. "I love you, Mrs. McCabe. You've given me everything missing from my life, and I can't imagine a life without you.''

"You won't have to. I'm not going anywhere.'' Sliding her hands around the collar of his shirt, she began unbuttoning his shirt. She gave him a sultry, upswept look full of sensual promise. "In fact, I think there's a little detail to our marriage that you need to attend to.''

He lifted a brow, but he was definitely interested. "Oh, and what's that?''

"Consummating it,'' she said huskily.

Desire heated his gaze. "Yes, ma'am.''

In a move that took her completely by surprise, he swept her into his arms, and she squealed in delight and clutched at his shoulders. Laughing, he headed toward the bedroom, and laid her gently on the mattress, following her down and settling beside her. All amusement ceased as he glided a hand beneath her blouse, and trailed his fingers over her rounded belly.

The spontaneous, but unmistakable kick beneath his palm startled them both. It was the first time Ford had felt the baby move.

"Oh," Grace said, her eyes wide. Ford chuckled warmly.

Leaning down, he placed a downy soft kiss on the spot where his daughter had kicked. "I love you, too," he assured her, then looked back up at Grace with a hopelessly-in-love grin.

The man was a marshmallow, and his baby hadn't even been born yet. Reaching out, Grace touched the crease in his cheek. "I hope she has your dimples."

He scooted back up and gazed reverently into her eyes. His fingers threaded through her hair, then he cupped the back of her head in his palm. "I already know she'll be as beautiful as you."

The man had a way with words, but at the moment, she didn't want to talk. Sensing her need to be intimately close, he kissed her leisurely, taking his time seducing her, until they were both breathless and anxious and naked. Hard, heated skin slid over soft, bare skin. Moans of pleasure mingled as Ford consummated their marriage in a ritual as old as time, and spent the night showing her the depths of his love for her.

In Ford's arms, Grace found heaven. Within his embrace, she experienced peace and contentment. And as his wife, she discovered complete fulfillment.

EPILOGUE

"TELL me the story again, Poppa," four-year-old Marie said, looking up at her grandfather with big round eyes the color of spring violets. Though she had her father's eyes, Marie had her mother's thick brown hair and delicate features. She was a beautiful combination of both of her parents.

From a doorway behind her father and daughter, Grace watched the two of them, keeping her presence a secret. There was something incredibly heartwarming in witnessing the bond between the pair, which had been evident since the moment Marie had been born. Since Dr. Chase had been on vacation when Grace had gone into early labor, Ellis Holbrook had delivered his grandchild. Grace would never forget the tears that had filled her father's eyes as he held the squalling baby in his hands, or her own husband's overjoyed expression when Ellis had informed them they had a perfect little girl. Together, the two men had cleaned her up and bundled her warmly, though it had been Ford's deep, crooning voice that had settled his daughter's cries.

Marie was crazy about Ford, and had her daddy wrapped around her little finger, as most little girls seemed to learn from the cradle. But Marie had a soft spot for her Poppa, too, and it seemed Ellis could deny his granddaughter nothing, either.

Ellis shifted the little girl on his knee, and smiled at her, making him look young and happier than

Grace could remember. "Aren't you tired of hearing the same old story, munchkin?"

"No." Marie snuggled against his broad chest, which was her way of telling him she wasn't going anywhere until she got what she wanted.

"Oh, all right." Ellis sighed, a sound of contentment, and leaned back in the recliner. His hand stroked the top of her head as he began the story that so captivated his granddaughter. "Once upon a time there lived a handsome prince, a beautiful princess and an evil stepfather..."

Grace heard a sound behind her and turned to see Ford approaching. She put a finger to her lips to keep him silent so they didn't disturb this precious moment, then crooked her finger at him to urge him to come to her. He did, slipping his arms around her waist from behind, and settling his splayed hands on her five-month-pregnant belly. His warmth and love surrounded her, and she reveled in how wonderful her life was.

Together, they stood there, listening to her father weave the fairy tale that had enchanted Marie since she was a one-year-old. Grace loved hearing this particular story just as much as her daughter did. It was her father's interpretation of her and Ford's courtship, with a mystical, magical spin to it. And each time Ellis told the tale, he made it more magnificent and imaginative than before. He combined fantasy with reality to create a whimsical fable of romance and adventure, complete with a sword fight between the evil stepfather and the handsome prince, and telling how the prince decided to spare the old man's life in exchange for his beautiful daughter. The evil stepfather became a good person, of course, and granted the prince his blessing as the young man swept the princess up onto his white steed and they rode off to their castle together.

The story left both Grace and Ford grinning. It was a lovely, charming rendition that put the past to rest for all of them.

Marie lifted her head, peering up at her grandfather's face, her eyes dancing with delight. "And then what happened, Poppa?"

Ellis pressed a kiss to the crown of Marie's head, and ended the story appropriately. "Why, they lived happily ever after, of course."

And they did.

HARLEQUIN® *Romance*®

Margot, *Shelby* and *Georgia*
are getting married. But first they have
a mystery to solve....

Join these three sisters on the way to the
altar in an exciting new trilogy from

BARBARA McMAHON

in Harlequin Romance

MARRYING MARGOT July 2000

A MOTHER FOR MOLLIE August 2000

GEORGIA'S GROOM September 2000

**Three sisters uncover secrets—
that lead to marriage with
the men of their dreams!**

HARLEQUIN®
Makes any time special ™

MAITLAND MATERNITY

Where the luckiest babies are born!

Join Harlequin® and Silhouette® for a special 12-book series about the world-renowned Maitland Maternity Clinic, owned and operated by the prominent Maitland family of Austin, Texas, where romances are born, secrets are revealed…and bundles of joy are delivered!

Look for
MAITLAND MATERNITY
titles at your favorite retail outlet, starting in August 2000

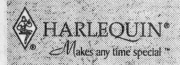
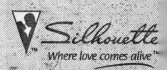

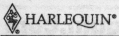
Coming Next Month

#3615 BACHELOR IN NEED Jessica Steele
Jegar Urquart needed Fennia's help in looking after his niece while
her parents were in hospital. Jegar clearly found Fennia attractive...
but while she could answer Jegar's need for a live-in nanny, Fennia
felt she must resist slipping into the role of live-in lover as well!

The Marriage Pledge

#3616 A MOTHER FOR MOLLIE Barbara McMahon
Patrick O'Shaunnessy can't help Shelby unravel her past—he's too
busy trying to run his investigative business and care for his little
girl! So Shelby suggests a temporary marriage: she'll look after his
daughter while he works for her. But Shelby starts wanting a more
permanent arrangement....

Beaufort Brides

#3617 THE FAITHFUL BRIDE Rebecca Winters
Years after Wade had called off their wedding, Janet found out why:
a friend had told him she was having an affair! Now Janet wanted
another wedding. She knew Wade would have no doubt of her
innocence come the honeymoon! But first she had to convince
him she was a bride worth trusting....

White Weddings

#3618 HIS DESERT ROSE Liz Fielding
When Prince Hassan al Rashid drew the world's media attention to
the abduction of well-known foreign correspondent Rose Fenton,
he also lost his heart. And, kidnapped by Hassan, Rose was
surprised to find that beneath the designer suit lay the heart of a
true desert prince!